SECRETS OF A PASTOR'S WIFE

BILLIE MIFF

Urban Aesop Presents

© 2017 Billie Miff

All rights reserved. No part of this publication may be reproduced in any form or by electronic or mechanical means, including information storage and retrieval systems without permission in writing from the publisher, except by a reviewer, who may quote a brief passage in reviews. First edition, December 25, 2017. Printed in the United States of America

This is a work of fiction. Names, characters, places and incidents either are products of the author's imagination or are used fictitiously. Any similarity to actual events or locales or persons, living or dead, is entirely coincidental.

Cover design: Adriane Hall

Edited by: K. Simone

Proofreader: Brandi Nevels

CHAPTER 1

Cookie

I ENTERED THE SANCTUARY THE SAME AS I ALWAYS DID every Sunday, full of hope and spirit that things would be different when I exited. The pastor was already in full swing delivering a valuable word. This goes to prove that our good Father will use any living vessel to be a messenger.

I took a little extra time to get the girls and myself together, hence the reason for my tardiness this morning. Usually, I am up early enough to meet with the other church sisters and deacons. Sometimes we can even make it to the Sunday school teachings by Deacon Radcliff. My youngest seemed to enjoy his stories. Today however, we made it just in time for the first scripture reading.

Like most of the women in our congregation, I donned one of my floral hats that accentuated my outfit. It was first Sunday, and the women used this as a way of competing with the other ladies. For me, dressing was just a part of who I am; there was no need to compete with anyone. For what? I had a husband who loved me, almost too much. But it still was more than these vultures could say.

Because my husband was the pastor, he was the object of a lot of attention. There was nothing like an attractive man of the cloth leading his flock to the truth. And I had no problem with his leadership in the House of the Lord. My problem was with the leadership in our household. Sure, every marriage has their share of problems, but ours surpassed what I expected. We don't have your typical marital situation.

From the way it appears, you would think we have the perfect marriage and happy family. However, that is just for the eyes of the public, which is so far from the truth. To avoid scorn and ridicule we keep up the façade, play a role on Sundays and for other church functions, just to make sure our cover isn't blown.

So, every time I entered in this place of worship, I'm torn, split inside spiritually and emotionally. Part of me felt the need to fulfill my duty as First Lady of the church and be supportive of my husband to the bitter end. Then there was the emotional side that was being submerged in a pool of discontentment. I am gasping for air and the water is rising all around me. The only place I can breathe freely is when I sit down in a pew. And even then, I have to look and listen to the source of my pain. Yet I grin and bear it, each and every Sunday morning.

Third row up to the left is where I sit. I am positioned towards the end of the pew, enough space for my two daughters and just enough room for Sister Jackson and her mini entourage to fill the rest of the area. She shows up with any number of guests. Some, I think come just to sample her cooking later in the afternoon.

The choir had us all on our feet with their soulful rendition of "Jesus is Real." Sometimes all it takes is some good praise and worship music to lift the spirit in the room. Our choir director, Lamont Jackson, was truly anointed. The energy he brought makes everyone want to shout for joy. He is a young musician with a true gift to lead and bring the best out of his members. Sister Jackson was his biggest fan, watching her son up there dancing, shouting, and praising could not make her any prouder.

It was nice to see her smiling again. Last year was a tough year for the Jackson Two. They were in the midst of turmoil within the church. Rumors had gotten out that Lamont was secretly dating the lead vocalist in the choir, Tarsha Wilson. At that time, Lamont was a keyboardist

Dating her wasn't the problem. There had been many inter-choir relationships, probably in every church. The issue surfaced when Tarsha announced to her mother that she was pregnant. What started out as a secret, ended up getting exposed by her mother when she approached Pastor Andrews demanding the dismissal of Lamont, not only from the choir, but the church as well. Of course that infuriated Sister Jackson and a feud ensued, blowing up into something newsworthy

After many public displays and verbal threats by the two matriarchs, Ms. Wilson decided to remove herself and her daughter from the church family they have known since Tarsha was christened there as an infant. She saw where the pastor wasn't willing to put his prize keyboard player out of the church under any circumstance. However, it all turned out for the best for Sister Jackson, with her being a single mother left to raise Lamont after his father was murdered due to gang violence. Her role has been tough especially with the various peer pressures that loom for a young man. In fact, Victory in Faith Baptist Church had been a saving grace for Sylvia Jackson and her son Lamont.

Pastor Carlton Andrews had taken on the position of mentor to so many young people but especially to this young man. It made them better. Lamont became more responsible, not only in the church family but as a new father. I have watched my husband change many lives for the better. That is what made him so adored by this faithful congregation. As the head of the church, he was doing his job. As the head of his household, well there is still much to be desired. From the outside looking in, you would never know the misery I lived in as the First Lady.

CHAPTER 2

Cookie

LIKE MOST WORKING AMERICANS, MY MONDAYS WERE crazy. I had a busy caseload with patients needing my undivided attention. Between my work as an LPN at the city's leading healthcare facility and my side hustle doing massage therapy, it seemed like I had to schedule time to breathe. I am always on the clock. Then I still have my motherly responsibilities when I return home from my hectic day.

Today, I had one more thing added to my already crowded agenda. My first counseling session was at 2 PM, which meant I had to cut one of my medical appointments short in order to make it there on time. If my marriage is worth saving, one of us had to take the first step.

"Mrs. Cooke, Ms. Stinson will see you now," said the young receptionist who interrupted my *Essence* magazine reading.

Taraji P. Henson had the feature this month and I was just finding out what my girl had going on. With movies, a hit television series, a new book coming out, sister girl had her life in order. If only I could get a grasp on mine.

Dr. Maxine Stinson was a pecan brown skinned woman in her late 30's. Her statuesque, curvy figure may have showed that she did some modeling in her day. If she didn't, she must have missed her calling.

"Mrs. Cooke, is it?"

"Actually, it's Andrews. Cooke is my maiden name. You can call me Sandra or Cookie. That's what my friends call me."

"I'm a bit confused. You booked your appointment under the name Cooke and not your married name?"

"My husband doesn't know that I'm here. So, I chose to remain anonymous."

"That right there says a whole lot. I guess we can start there. Why keep counseling a secret from him, Sandra?"

"We just don't see eye to eye on some things."

"Some things?"

"OK, a lot of things. He really does not believe we need counseling. At least that's what he said when I approached him on the subject."

"So, he doesn't feel you guys are having problems?"

"I mean he knows things between us are a bit rocky but not to the level where he thinks we need to go to a counselor. He says we shouldn't put our faith in outsiders."

"Oh wow. There's something deeper going on here."

"It gets deep, Ms. Stinson."

"Please, you can call me Maxine."

"Carlton or Carl as I call him, my husband, is the pastor of a well-known church. He is a extremely popular man in many different circles. His reputation means a lot to him."

"More than his marriage?"

"It seems that way at times."

"Do you two have children together?"

"Yes, we do." She noticed the look on my face right away.

"Why that look? Did I say something inappropriate?"

"Of course not. It's just that's another subject of concern. A can, I don't care to open."

"If it's too much, we don't have to go in that direction right now. But for you to discuss what the issues are, we must dive into the root. That means going some places you may not feel comfortable going."

"Well, it takes me back to the beginning of our marriage when we decided to have a child. I wanted to be the type of wife that's supportive and attentive of her husband's needs."

"What was the beginning like for you?"

This was a subject that I honestly never thought I'd have to retell. They say that therapy heals the heart. I hope that opening up to Maxine helps in my healing process. The experience alone was traumatic. Making it through that time in my life was by God's grace.

"When I first met Carl, I was a battered woman. I had just endured a physically abusive relationship which had me so anti-men that I didn't ever think I would be in a meaningful relationship again."

"It's a shame that women have to go through something just to find someone for them," she sympathized.

"My faith in men was virtually shattered. I had a heart to heart with my mother and she encouraged me to seek God for my healing."

"That sounds like a motherly thing to say."

"Well, she relies so much on her church upbringing, that's all she knows. I took her advice and started attending bible study at a local church, Victory in Faith. Getting in the word was refreshing for my soul, not to mention that bible study nights got me out of the house after falling into a brief depression. It didn't take long for my serenity to be interrupted by man's innate nature to assert themselves on the opposite sex. During one of our Wednesday bible study classes, I noticed a change in how the pastor and associate pastor were conducting the service. Afterwards, that Wednesdays got even more interesting. First, Associate Pastor Gerald Pryor made it his business to offer himself as my personal escort to my car. On the way, he expressed his interest in getting to know me better. His approach was subtle and quite innocent. Kind of caught me off guard because with him being so dedicated to his teachings, I never figured him to be a pursuer of women. Part of me wasn't taking his attempts seriously, mostly because I was feeling less than attractive at that time. My skin was still in the healing process from bruises left on my upper arms and neck area. The physical abuse I had suffered left its mark in more ways than one. For a man to show signs of attraction towards me, tended to get lost in the translation."

"Can definitely relate to that."

I wondered how, but continued, nonetheless.

"His actions caught the attention of his mentor and lead, Pastor Carlton Andrews, so much so that he was adamant about knowing his young protégé's intentions. When I told him that he was just speaking to me on general subject matter, nothing too deep, he surprised me by his reaction. He instantly pulled out the charm card and started to try his luck. Carlton was a little different. He still remained true to his position as pastor and teacher; he just let it be known that he was more knowledgeable about the word than his counterpart."

"No, he didn't use that angle, did he?"

"He sure did, but that wasn't the half. Carl invited me out to an honest meeting over dinner to discuss scripture. It did interest me to get some insight on a one-on-one basis from someone as learned as the pastor. That date turned to an afternoon at the harbor, then we were meeting for lunch on my break from work."

"He swooned you," she teased.

And I had to chuckle to myself as I remembered that time.

"Yes, if you want to call it that. We were enjoying each other's company and it was a refreshing change from the men I was used to."

"Sounds like he was just what you needed."

"That's what my mom thought as well. In fact, she was emphatic about me sticking with this man. 'It's hard to find a man of the cloth that's as young and handsome as he is' she would repeatedly tell me, like she was his biggest fan."

"And he passed the 'mom test' too? So, what went wrong?"

"Well, things were moving along smoothly. Carl played his position and made me forget all about Gerald, the associate pastor. Bible studies progressed to Sunday services, where I would hear him preach with such conviction that the spirit inside drew me nearer; not only to God, but to him also. We began an exclusive relationship, vowing to be obedient to the word. The most affection we displayed in public was mostly holding hands, only engaging in a respectful kiss at the end of our dates."

"Wow, that's impressive."

"We maintained that way of living for a little over three years. It was our way of getting to know the other person fully without the threat of intimacy clouding things. I learned things about Carlton that I never knew. The closer we got the more he opened up."

"In what ways?"

"Carl suffers from a digestive tract syndrome which has plagued him throughout his adult years. It was tough for him to even explain how the illness has affected him. He has been medicated and even endured surgery that has left him with abnormal scar on his abdominal area.

He says it makes for difficult digestion and embarrassing restroom moments."

"Wow. I commend him for even being comfortable enough to share that with you; someone who had never experienced that."

"It really bonded us, yet I still didn't know how it was going to affect me. I grew to love Carl nevertheless and we decided to take our union to the marriage level. This is when I noticed a change inside. Everyone around me was so happy for me finally renewing my spirit and putting my past relationships behind me, I started feeling pressure to love Carlton 'for better or for worse, til death do us part'."

"Isn't that what being marriage is about? You vow to love each other through whatever, forever?"

"Don't get me wrong, I do love him. However, at that time, I had doubts questioning whether I was actually in love with this man. With the previous failures, I never learned the difference between loving someone and being in love. Those in my past called themselves loving me but showed me, in other ways, that they didn't deserve my love in return. Now, here was a man loving me in a different way, and I wasn't sure how to love him back. I thought maybe intimacy would ease my uncertainty and prove that I had made the right decision marrying this man, however, it turned out much different. Our honeymoon was supposed to be happiest time of my life; the union between husband and wife, made complete by consummation. After a wedding that lacked the 'IT' factor that all women dream about, I figured the night would be everything I anticipated. Now remember, I had never seen this man naked, nor had he seen me. Only in my mind had I imagined being with him, so there was a wide range of emotions flowing through me. When the moment finally came, I was as anxious as a teenager losing her virginity to her high school sweetheart. In essence, it was a similar situation. I had committed myself to celibacy during our courting period. So, in the bathroom as I put on my sexiest lingerie, all that crossed my mind was would Carl find me as sexy as I felt."

"I see."

"I exited the bathroom, walking seductively over to the bed where my brand-new husband awaited me with wanting eyes. This was the first time I saw lust in him, but it was alright because his lust for me was accepted and something he knew he didn't have to repent over. Half of his body was covered by the comforter, leaving his chest and broad shoulders exposed. He moved to come out of the bed, but I could sense his apprehension. For some reason, I thought it was me or something that he saw that he wasn't pleased with. The closer I got, the more he fidgeted with the covers, positioning himself deeper in the bed."

"The lights were off but the bright Bahamian moon casted a glow in our beach front bungalow. There was just enough illumination to see all his features, especially his facial expressions. What I saw in his visage was self-consciousness. But for what, I wondered."

"I held him under the covers, and he held me back. We kissed and my hands began to explore his body. My questions were answered when my fingers ran across a rigid area on his skin that nearly frightened me to the touch. I quickly moved from there and made believe that I hadn't touched him in that place. Problem was, he knew it and I knew it too. It did something to me. I tried with all my might to block it out and make love to a man I vowed to love for the rest of my life, but my mind just couldn't focus on giving or receiving pleasure."

"Oh, that must have not been a pleasant feeling."

"No, in fact, I felt awful. I couldn't believe I was having a difficult time being intimate with my newly wedded husband on our honeymoon. I mean, who does that? What my fingers felt etched a vision in my head as we engaged in our first sexual experience. Closing my eyes did not change a thing as my attraction was tainted by my own conscience. I couldn't shake it. And instead of feeling immense pleasure at the conclusion, I had a sense of relief when it was over. In fact, I cried and for a variety of reasons. He really couldn't help what he was dealing with no more than I could help how it was impacting me."

"When I woke the next morning, Carl was in the bathroom washing his face. The door was partially open, enough for me to see his body in the light. His scar and whole stomach area were now in full view. This was my first real sight of my husband and here I was literally trying to process it. He turned and caught me staring and immediately shame consumed me. I started to question everything about myself, about this. The biggest question was what was God trying to show me?"

"I'm speechless, Sandra. There's so much to digest. Just too much for this one session. I'll need you to come back. I mean, that's if you want to."

"I think this was good for me. But I must warn you though. It gets deeper, way more real."

"I believe I can handle it."

"You say that now."

'Cookie, I'm a trooper."

"We'll see. I'll set up an appointment."

When I pulled into our driveway, I felt a wave of guilt come over me like I had been whitewater rafting. This was nothing new. It seemed like every day when I come home from work, or any place for that matter, I dreaded going inside fearing what I am about to face. On one hand, I love the feeling of warmth I get from my daughters, Sherice and Chloe. Yet in the blink of an eye, the mood in the house switches to gloom all because of Carl's spirit.

For their sake I endure a lot. As a mother, it is my responsibility to be the buffer for my kids. Parenting is a mutual job, so it frustrates me to no end when Carl and I are not on the same page with the girls. Sacrifices are supposed to be made to make them better, and it's just not an even playing field in our household. This is what adds to the friction. I would have never thought a man so committed to uniting his church family would not put forth the same energy to keeping his own family together. When I mentioned that we should go to counseling to address our issues, all that did was stir up a huge argument and created even more tension. I think I will keep my visit to Dr. Maxine Stinson quiet for a while.

CHAPTER 3

Cookie

"You still haven't told me how your children got introduced to your marital issues."

Maxine was looking stunning this afternoon. She had the glow of a woman that was full of life. Her mocha brown skin glistened in the afternoon sun that peeked its way through the venetian blinds in her office. She was dressed conservatively in a silk sleeveless top and some linen dress slacks. For me, I felt under dressed in my work scrubs.

"My daughters seem to always find a way into our sorted mix. It's not by their doing or mine."

"Your husband involves them?"

"Yes, but that is nothing new. From the start, there has always been this 'thing.'"

"What do you mean?"

"As a couple, your hope is to have children and live a

happy life. So, even though my wedding and honeymoon was less than desirable, I still wanted to be a mother in the worst way."

"That's natural in any woman. Giving birth is one of the greatest joys of life. I don't have any children but too many mothers have shared with me those special moments."

"My mother, Ms. Della Mae Cooke, used to sit me down as a little girl and explain to me about her joys and pains of motherhood. She would tell me how a woman is supposed to be obedient to her mate, catering to and satisfying his needs. These things stuck with me through the years, and I tried to live by those principles in my relationships. As a wife, I knew that becoming a mother was the natural order of things."

"With Carl and I just starting out, I figured a love child between us would bond us together and make us strong enough to fight any battle that comes our way. When I became pregnant and throughout the months leading up to the delivery, Carl was supportive at times then suddenly distant. I didn't really question his behavior because I was going through mood changes as well. Then after the birth of Sharice, my mood transformed into pure love and admiration for our beautiful baby girl. She had a mixture of his features and mine, so she definitely had our genes. Young Sharice was giving off such radiance that it should have been automatic to express love towards her. Now me, I was full of baby weight and in desperate need of recovery time, but our daughter was faultless."

"Of course. Once you made that decision to become a mother, it happens."

"Carl surprised me by how much he was changing, not only towards me but Sharice too. There were times he would be downright cold and emotionless then sometimes he was truly kind and adoring. I couldn't put my finger on it but there was something wrong. The older Sharice or Reecie as I affectionally called her, the more aware she became of the world around her. She knew the difference between mommy and daddy, choosing for herself where she wanted to place her affection. More times than he cared to admit, Reecie would cling to me. Normally, little girls are in favor of the male parent, yet in our case it was just the opposite. Reecie loved her daddy, but she was a mommy's girl to the heart."

"Carl took offense to that and it showed in his mood around the house. I mean a small child in their first few years needs to go through the natural maturing process. The parent's guide and should understand that there will be subtle to extreme changes in the child. Carl refused to believe that Reecie was entering into different phases in her young life. It was almost like he was showing resentment, which to me was a sign of regret that I even had her."

"Around Sharice's fourth year, Carl and I discussed bringing another child into our home. Because he introduced it to me, I was excited about the possibility of motherhood again. To my astonishment, Carl suggested that we try adoption to become parents to a child with unfortunate circumstances. As a new mother and supportive wife, there was not even a second thought about considering his request. I was still able to bear children, however, because he wanted to try this route, I went with it."

"We had our heart set on a baby boy. My heart was truly ready to welcome a little man into our world. The adoption agency was immensely helpful assisting us with our search. We looked through a number of photos and reviewed various family situations until we found the right situation. Or so we thought."

"There was a small boy, maybe 14 or 15 months old, that Carl and I fell in love with. Evidently, the young mother who had him was hooked on heroin really bad and gave him up for adoption claiming she didn't have time to be a mother. Now, the story itself melted our hearts and we immediately wanted to be a parent to the baby. Then at the last hour, the grandparents contacted the agency and decided that they would take over custody. The whole experience was tough to deal with and it tore us up inside."

"After that ordeal, I assumed our search was over. Months had passed without as much as a discussion about whether we would consider the adoption process again. Then one day I overheard Carl on a phone conversation with someone from the agency. I didn't read too much into it, figuring it was just a follow up call. It totally shocked me when he came home from work with a little girl in tow. I hadn't come home yet so imagine what was on my mind when I saw her on our sofa sitting next to him."

"Oh my God, Sandra. I can't believe he would go and do that without even consulting with you." Maxine was astonished as I was, never thinking he would be that thoughtless, especially your husband.

"And he did. In fact, he had the nerve to be in there playing with her as if they had a kindred spirit. He introduced Chloé, who was almost three years older than Sharice. I thought having a big sister would be good for her, but I was so wrong. Instead of our unit getting closer, Chloé moved tighter to her father and showed more resentment towards Sharice, and especially me. I could not understand what I'd done to make her feel that way. She would talk back, roll her eyes, basically just very defiant. However, when she was around Carl she acted like a perfect angel. It was literally like night and day, so much that Carl wouldn't believe me when I would tell him how she was behaving."

"Sounds like that little girl has done that before," Maxine expressed.

"I definitely had to do some research on little Miss Chloé. I decided to call the family services agency and ask a few questions about the family that had put Chloé up for adoption. They told me that the children in that home were split up because the living environment was unstable. The mother was left to raise three kids after her husband chose to end their marriage then move to another state to live with another woman and her family. The mother just couldn't handle the financial burden."

"That's a shame those kids had to suffer like that, all because that man took the easy way out," she lamented.

"What it did to Chloé was make her a very bitter child, and her relationship with her mother was severed, making her feel loveless. You'd think she would be angry towards men the way her dad abandoned them, but she actually had moved closer to the new man in her life which happens to be my husband."

"How is your relationship with Chloé now? She's a bit older. Surely she has made some progress."

"I wish I could say that we go shopping together and talk about boys like a regular mother/daughter pairing but that just isn't the case. There are days where she will accept the love and advice I offer. I try and teach her things like basic female attributes that a young woman should know growing into womanhood. I believe that's my responsibility as a mother and would be doing her a disservice if I didn't at least make an attempt. But she's young and she has a lot of rebellion in her. One of the main issues I'm concerned with is her attitude rubbing off on Reecie's innocence."

"What are they like together?"

"Chloé has embraced the role of big sister which I applaud her for. I keep a close eye on them, however. Sharice is my biological daughter. The genes inside of her determine her personality. Chloé, on the other hand, came from dysfunction and carried that aura in with her suitcases. What we are trying to develop as a family is unknown to her. She is a teenager now, a whole new set of challenges for us. She has become very crafty in manipulating situations. My eyes are wide open. Carl can trust his little darling, but I don't."

"You guys have an interesting home life. What do you think will help make the environment better?"

"Only the grace of God."

CHAPTER 4

Cookie

IT WAS EARLY ON SATURDAY MORNING WHEN I entered the kitchen to fix a cup of hot tea. Carl was at the table, sitting in a chair with Reecie on a small stool between his legs getting her hair braided. During those years in our marriage, he had shown beautician skills. Nothing professional but he could pursue the trade if he chose to. Of course, pastoring a church is his calling and he would never go against that.

I looked out the window and saw the neighbors on our street getting their lawnmowers prepped for a day of grass maintenance. It looked like a pit stop at a NASCAR event, the way they were tuning, oiling, and gassing up their machines. Whether it was riders or push behinds, these guys were pumped for some horticultural competition.

This was the scene every weekend. All the lawns in our neighborhood were immaculate; it is what trademarks your property and one of the selling points that brought us here. Life was different in Delaware; a change and new way of living was good for us. Bowie, Maryland became our resting place, and the welcoming community made this home for us.

Victory in Faith Baptist Church was located in the heart of Bowie, right up the street from the high school, on Annapolis Road. Carl came highly recommended from the work he had done for the community in Delaware. It was widely recognized in Christian publications with distribution reaching all the way to Virginia. When their pastor took a position in another church in Oxon Hill it left a void that Carl was destined to fill.

We have enjoyed living here in Bowie. Now I just wish the harmony outside our home would come inside and make its presence known. The silence in the kitchen was a clear indicator of what the mood was like in the Andrews household.

"How do you like your hair sweetheart?" Carl asked Reecie, after completing the arduous task of braiding her thick locks. She didn't reply right away, but the facial expression she gave me told it all. Evidently her silence was enough of an answer for Carl because he got up abruptly.

"Maybe your mother will have the time to do it over, if that makes you happy." His response was so immature, and I showed my displeasure.

"Carl, if she wanted me to do it, I would've done it. But you insisted on being the one, so don't be mad if she doesn't like one of your creations."

"I'm not mad," he spat out.

"It sure sounds like it. I can't tell who's the child and who's the adult."

I know that was pretty low of me to say, but it is the truth. My statement must have struck a nerve because Carl stormed out of the kitchen without saying another word. Was I sorry for hurting his feelings? A little. But I do not regret letting him have it.

This was not the first time I had to show another side of myself in the house. Carl had a way of touching a nerve and for whatever reason I reacted in a manner that is not always pleasant. This kept tension in the air as thick as London Fog. In fact, what I am fearing is our marital issues turning into a cancer that can't be cured.

Reecie always felt trapped in the middle, which made me feel horrible. She loved her daddy immensely; however, she is at a stage in her life where she is embracing her womanhood. My job is to lead her in the right direction in terms of her femininity, yet Carl still felt the need to hold on to his little girl for dear life. This contrast of feelings towards Reecie is not good for her growth.

"Mommy, what did I do wrong?" Reecie asked innocently.

"You didn't do anything wrong, sweetheart. Why do you think that?"

"Because daddy got upset and left out."

"That's just your father. I don't think he meant anything by it."

"I don't like seeing you guys fighting." She was

breaking my heart and making me even more pissed at Carl for making her feel that way.

"Baby don't confuse our disagreements as fights. Adults will have differences from time to time. Believe me, we're ok."

I thought I was doing my best to convince myself that we are alright, but deep inside I knew we needed help. I recognized it first and that's probably why he's so apprehensive about going to counseling. He had his notions that counselors get paid to listen to us talk about things we already know about ourselves. Add that to the list of our disagreements.

I pulled into the church's parking lot and noticed Carl's car parked in his usual spot. Instantly my mood had changed from cheerful to gloomy. I did not like how he had that kind of power over my emotions. After his mini tantrum he threw in the kitchen earlier, I was determined to make the best of my day.

We had this mandatory board of directors meeting, so I put on my best smile and walked in with the confidence of a runway model. I am the First Lady, empowered by God Almighty himself. That is the attitude I had to exude just to keep my sanity. Besides, no one in our church family knows what we are going through, so if he can keep our cover, I can too.

"Glad you all could make it today. I know it's your Saturday afternoon and you could be doing many other things, so I appreciate your presence."

Everyone in the room just nodded then let Carl continue.

"First on the agenda, is there any old business that needs to be tabled? Any concerns that anyone wants to discuss?"

Brother Wilcox spoke first, breaking the ice. "If I may, Pastor Andrews, request that our choir director rearrange the men's choir. No offense to Brother Braxton, but he is throwing off the whole tenor section with his offbeat swaying."

We all had to chuckle because it was true. I noticed it, just didn't know anyone else did.

"I've seen what you're speaking about. When I looked at the tapes from recent services, the main choir was fluid, but the men's choir did not measure up." Carl stated flatly. "We'll make some changes."

"Thank you, Pastor."

"Since we're talking about the choir, I want to introduce something the deacons and I have been discussing; the starting of a children's praise team displayed through dance."

My eyes nearly bucked out of my head when I heard Carl's ingenious idea. Not because he was introducing something so innovative. No, it was the fact that I brought the idea up just about a month ago. He thought it would not work and dismissed it as a meaningless concept. Now, all of a sudden, it's his brainchild. I couldn't believe his nerve and I knew that he could see the disgust in my body language. That's why he kept avoiding eye contact.

"Let's see, I have some other news. We are instituting a prison ministry here at Victory. The bible says,

'When I was in prison, did you visit me?' Well, it's our duty to go and minister the word to those behind the walls who are in desperate need of a word of hope. Maybe we can develop some messengers for those men lost serving time."

Lost? I don't think Carl even realized that he indirectly insulted those incarcerated. They may be doing time, but I hardly believe that they are lost.

"Sister Andrews, I'd like for you to put a team together to go into the prison system and deliver the word."

"Huh, me? I mean...yes, of course. I think it will be quite an experience."

"Good, good. I'm glad you're motivated."

I was boiling inside and couldn't wait until we got home. I wasn't going to show my ass up here at the church. I wouldn't give him the pleasure of seeing me in that light. However, home is fair game. Motivated? I'll show him just how motivated I am to pour hot coals over him verbally.

"Well, if there isn't anything else, enjoy the rest of your day."

Everyone began to exit the room and as I gathered my things, I felt his eyes seething down at me.

"You have some nerve," I said as I left the room without saying another word. All I wanted to do was to get home.

Momma's car was sitting in the driveway when I pulled up. I sure was glad to see her. Lately we haven't had much time to talk. My mother and I have a strange relationship; sometimes we're good, other times we just exist as mother-daughter. But overall, the love is there and undeniable.

"So how have you been, my dear?" Momma asked as we sat down to a cup of tea.

"Oh, I don't know. Where do I start, Dell?"

My mother, Della Mae Cooke, has always had my back and has been more like a friend than a mother for the better part of my life. Because she had me at an early age, we can relate on most topics, yet disagree like sisters on certain things too. When she gets in "check-up" mode, I often refer to her by her first name, as if we're old girlfriends.

"A lot is going on around here. I just try my best daily to keep the peace."

"Well, Cookie, you know what I always say, 'When in doubt, go to church.'"

"Church? That's just adding to the drama."

"But how? It's supposed to be a place to leave your burdens."

"It seems that those burdens I leave there develop legs and follow me home."

"I don't understand."

I wanted so badly to go into detail about the events that took place today, yesterday, or even the last week for that matter, but Ms. Della has been pro Carl Andrews since the day I introduced them. The fact that I was dating a pastor could not have tickled her more. She looked at him like he was the saving grace for her baby girl. After back-to-back abusive relationships, it was hard for her to see me with those kinds of men. Saying anything to discredit Pastor Carl Andrews would be blasphemy to her ears. To her, he can do no wrong, which made me feel like she put him above me. It had always been that way throughout our marriage, and it produced a mini gap between us. In fact, the more sanctified she became over the years, the more she leaned in his favor.

"For me, it surpasses all understanding. Besides, if I told you the truth, the walls of Jericho would come crashing down."

"What does that mean?"

She knew the scripture. If I sing loud enough these walls will collapse freeing me from the drama. For now, I'll keep my issues to myself. In time hopefully things will change.

"Never mind, momma. Nothing for you to worry about."

CHAPTER 5
Adrian

"Ok gentlemen roll call! Listen for your name then respond with your M.D.C. number. Bed #9, Upshaw, Adrian! State your number!" the burly guard barked out with his cap pulled down tightly over his bald head.

To most, his tone and appearance would be intimidating, but not me. I've seen guys like him for years doing the same thing. Correctional officers are typical, using size and military style commands to get their point across.

"1099053, present," I answered confidently. And with that minor formality I returned to my daily routine of folding laundry, neatly placing it in the small locker where I kept all my possessions.

Routines are what get you by while doing time. For over 15 years of my life, I have endured the struggles of incarceration by keeping to myself and sticking to the script. The script varies from person to person as everybody does time differently. Some like confrontation, always getting into it with prison guards, then some stay in people's business and eventually become informants or "snitches" as they are called on the inside. That's considered hard time. I prefer to do mine stress free, play my lane, only resorting to aggression when there is a violation of space or property.

Those are the rules and there are many to adhere to behind the walls. The number one rule is if you see something going on, act like you didn't see anything going on. In other words, stay in your own lane on the highway. The less you know, the better off you will be. There have been plenty of people who have gotten severely hurt by witnessing an incident then running around talking about what they saw. What you think is said in secret always ends up leaking out, usually to the wrong people.

Another unwritten rule is don't get seen associating too close with prison administration. In the prison world, perception generally trumps reality. What may appear as an innocent word with the Warden, to the onlookers it would most likely come off as information being given. Snitching is assumed before anything is ever confirmed. It is best to watch your clandestine conversations with officials because anything can be left to interpretation. Bad things can happen when you're on the losing side of circumstance.

"A.U., are you going to yard? You know the ballers are all going out today."

"Yeah, I'm heading out there, but I may not play today."

"C'mon, brah, why not? We need a point guard out there."

"Just don't feel it today. I'm probably going to run a few miles around the track. Got some things on my mind."

"I feel you, brah. Come get down if you change your mind."

"Bet that."

As I made my way around the track surrounding the big yard, I thought about how drastically my life has changed over the past 15 years. This may sound cliché, but it really does seem like yesterday that I was in society, breathing natural air. It is amazing how in the blink of an eye the world as you know it can be turned upside down.

Everything I had going on in my life, was lost with one bad decision. I should have just said "No" when I was asked if I could help them out. These guys acted as if they were my friends, so I didn't think assisting them would do me any harm. Boy was I wrong.

I was well past the two-mile mark on the track, breezing by the guys on the court. My thoughts were racing keeping pace with my stride, simultaneously jogging my memory to the night when all control was lost. Sometimes knowing the right people can lead you down the wrong path.

On the street, I was always someone who was associated to somebody important. Guess what that made me?

Somebody important. People would want to be in your presence just to get next to your associates for their own benefit. That's what happened to me and became my downfall.

I was working for this telecommunications company up in northern Maryland, near Towson just south of Baltimore. There was a coworker who was around my age, everyone else was in their mid-30's and 40's. With us being 25 and 26 respectively, instantly we formed a bond. We got cool when the company had this training program for a new position, and we were grouped together with a few women. All of us really thought this was a golden opportunity to move up within the company, which meant more money of course.

After a month in this program, it seemed like the process wasn't leading anywhere. Corey was just as frustrated as I was, he was more vocal about it, questioning our supervisors about the delay in the pay raise they promised. We carpooled back and forth to work a couple times and I could tell he was stressing about some money issues.

"Adrian, you interested in making some extra money?" Corey asked breaking the silence on our way home from work.

"Of course, I am. That's why I'm hoping they hurry up and finish this boring training we have to go through. It's too much just to get a dollar and some change raise in pay."

"I know. I was looking for a way to come up with

some cash in the meantime. I'm gonna need your help though."

"What you up to, Corey?"

"I remember you telling me about some friends of yours who deal on the black market."

"Yeah, them boys are into a lot of things."

"Does Brian still work at that coat factory where they have all those furs?"

"Yes, he does, why?"

"Well, I know that there has to be some of them furs that are defective and they discard them. I'd like to buy them. I'm sure I can get top dollar on resell."

"Let me guess. You want me to talk to him for you."

"Basically, I really want you to put us together so we can work a deal and I'll cut you in on what I make."

"I can set you guys up with a meeting."

Brian and Corey met to discuss a deal for some of the damaged furs from the store. They came to a mutual price on the goods and they even came up with a scheme to acquire the furs from the factory. Brian told me about their plans and all he needed me to do was to show him where the shop was.

The night Corey came through to pick me up had me with mixed feelings. I guess because I didn't know enough about the details of what was going on. That made me a bit leery. The business was between them, so I was glad my role was limited. All I had to do was ride with Corey over to meet Brian. Real easy.

I had no idea that things would change for the worst once we got there. When we arrived, I directed Corey a little over 2 miles. The guys were still on the court going at it. My partner Tree, who is about 6'5, went up for a dunk and got clobbered by Muscle Head, who weighs about 205 in solid muscles. Evidently, he was not having any free baskets today. Bragging rights were on the line and nobody wanted to get shined on, especially in front of the young female officers out watching the yards activities.

Some trash talking ensued between the two competitors. The talk escalated to some shoves and pushes. Officers had their radios in hand in anticipation of a potential scuffle. Before they would call a "10-10" which signaled a fight, they had to assess the situation. A few of the teammates stepped in and restored order. They then resumed the game and ran a couple more points before yard ended.

"We sure could've used you out there today, A.U."

"Had a lot on my mind. I was in no condition to play ball. Running was the best thing for me."

"Yeah, we saw you out there doing a 10k," Pimp joked.

"Naw, almost 3 miles."

"Well, whatever it was must've been heavy. You know where to drop your burdens off, don't you?"

"Where Preach?"

"Out there at the trash pick-up for Old Man Smitty to put in one of his socks," Slim ZO interjected always looking for a laugh.

"No, fool, church. Take your problems to the altar,

my brother. I promise you'll feel a load lifted. A clean soul will make your time go a little easier."

Preacher man was always trying to recruit guys to go to church with him. He doesn't do it in a pushy way, so I respect his attempts.

"I don't really do church, Preach," I stated.

"That's good because all you have to do is show up and let church do you. What you got to lose?"

"We'll see. Maybe one of these days I'll give it a shot."

"Don't let something drastic happen that forces you there. It's better that you go voluntarily."

"That's probably what it'll take, something drastic," I stated flatly.

"Alright, be careful what you ask for. It just may come your way."

CHAPTER 6

Cookie

"I swear, Max, I don't know what to do with her."

"Cookie, teenagers are definitely a handful."

"She is way more than a handful. The lies, the deceit, the sneakiness, I don't know which is worst. And to think, I have another daughter who is not too far behind her in age and witnessing all of this."

"Is Reecie giving you trouble too?"

"Oh no. But I'm afraid that Chloe will influence her. She's now starting to look at Chloe with admiration, from the way she dresses to her mannerisms. I even heard her repeating some of the little trendy sayings that the kids say to be cool. I'm just worried. Am I taking things too far?"

"Not at all. It's natural to be concerned about our kids. What does Carl have to say about all of this?"

"Carl is so passive in his approach to parenting. I

guess that's how Chloe gets away with so much. To her, dealing with him is like a free pass. She has definitely learned the art of manipulation, where she got it, I don't know."

"Some things don't have to be taught by parents, kids are picking up habits outside the home, in school or other places where they hang."

"Or from the company they keep, like teenage boys they have no business being with. Especially when I've warned her of the dangers."

"Whoa, Cookie! Where is all this coming from?"

"Well, I kinda stumbled across Chloe's phone the other day ---,"

"Kinda stumbled?" I believe Max was reading through my cloudiness.

"Ok, I was snooping through her phone and saw that she had been in frequent contact with an older boy, and I have major concerns with that."

"Did you see anything that leads you to think that something was going on?"

"No, but from personal experience, I've seen bad things happen with older boys at that age."

"Oh really, this might be a deeper issue that may need to be discussed. Care to share?"

"It was so long ago and very complicated, but I believe it started a cycle that was hard to break."

"Please continue."

I began to recount that horrible period in my life that I tried desperately to erase.

"Oh Terry... oh Terry. C'mon, baby right there. Give

it to me." And he did just that by upping his aggressive sexual nature to the tenth power. He started gyrating and driving into me like he was auditioning for a porn movie. It got to the point where pleasure turned to pain in the blink of an eye.

"Ouch, Terry! You're hurting me."

"Shut up bitch! This is what you've been asking for. Walking around here in all that tight stuff. You're such a tease."

"I wasn't wearing that to tease you. I thought you liked how I dressed?"

"Look, I'm not trying to talk about that right now. I'm just trying to get my nut and get off you." I couldn't believe he had the audacity to look me in the face and talk to me like that. I've never felt so empty.

There were good moments though. Terrence Allen would often do romantic things to woo me. Send flowers to my job, spontaneous getaways, even little tokens of affection that expressed his love for me. I had no doubt that there was a future with this man. Then things went left. Terry revealed another side of his enigmatic personality, one that involved drug usage.

Cocaine was his drug of choice. The day he brought it into our household was the day fear entered into me. I literally saw him change from the sweet man who wanted me to look at him as a king, to a man falling fast from the throne. His attitude became nasty towards people, especially me, and his patience was noticeably short.

One day, while using, he caught me staring at him

with disgust. Instead of embarrassment his anger rose, and fire filled his eyes.

"What the fuck you looking at? I ain't no side show. C'mere, Cookie," he demanded. I was reluctant to join him, now thinking back, I should've never gone over to that sofa. Again, fear was a willing ménage `a' trois in our relationship when he was on the powder. Against what I was feeling, I slid in next to him not knowing what to expect.

"Here, try some of this, since you're so interested in what I'm doing." I'd never had any experience with drugs, I mean smoked a little weed here and there growing up but nothing heavy like the white stuff. At that moment I was feeling the pressure from him. He separated some of the powdery substance from the small pile on the coffee table then drew a small line with a playing card, leaning down, opened one nostril and snorted the entire line into his nose as if that were training 101. When he came up, he gave me a menacing glare, then he nodded to me.

"Terry, I'm fine really." I thought being honest would make him back off a little.

"Girl, if you don't taste this!" he raised his hand as if he was gonna back hand slap me. I cringed then an uncontrollable shake came down upon me. Part of it was fear, the other was uncertainty of what would be the effects of my first foray with cocaine. Before I could blink t, Terry quickly gripped the back of my head with his large hand and forcefully pushed me towards the table and another line he'd drawn out. "It'll make you feel better, Cook, you'll see."

Still shaking I held one nostril closed as he did and took in half the line with one swift sniff, leaned my head back and felt a burning sensation inside. "C'mon, you're wasting my shit," he proceeded to clean up what I left. I sat there froze letting it take its course over my body. It was obvious that his senses were immune to the coke, my mind, however, was reeling at the speed of light. Before I knew what was happening, Terry began groping me, tugging at my bra from the front then snatching it off. I sat there allowing him to have his way, no resistance at all.

I was stimulated by his rough touch. It turned me on somehow. Climbing on his lap, I ended up giving him the ride of his life, enjoying it immensely myself. Afterwards, once we both released all our tension, I seemed to erase his abusive actions from my memory. Instead, I replaced it with the feeling of bliss and pleasure we had just experienced.

I ended up becoming addicted to the cocaine, the sex under the influence of the drug, and the control Terry had over me. He took care of all our expenses, when I got paid from work, I kept everything, all I had to do was please him and keep my mouth shut. His drug transactions were enough to support our habit and keep our lifestyle intact. A little verbal abuse every now and again was worth the sacrifice.

It wasn't until Terry started taking things to another level. He became even more aggressive with his tone and his actions towards me. When there was a drought in the area and product was scarce, somehow that was my fault. Suddenly, being the drug dealer's girlfriend wasn't what I wanted. I was in too deep though; he had too much power over me. I tried to make him happy by giving into his sexual wishes. Gave him oral pleasure whenever he desired, acted out his pornographic fantasies, even new positions, anything to ease his anger.

That did not seem to be enough. The sex became harder to bear and by not adhering to his demands, he would hit me with closed fist punches to places like my ribs, legs, or arms so the bruises weren't visible. That way I could still go to work and nothing would seem out of the norm. Financially, things changed too. He was no longer using his money to support us. In fact, he was losing money left and right and I was looked at to fill in the void of income. If I didn't agree, lord be on my side that day. I could end the night being raped, physically abused or both.

I could not keep living like that, so I went to my Mom, Della, for help but as usual her answer for me was, "Baby, you need to go to church." What was church going to do for me when I went back home? I had a bible right in my nightstand. In fact, I could have a mattress laying on a stack of bibles and that wouldn't stop him from whooping or raping me. I despised Terry for what he did and I feared for my life.

I decided enough was enough, when Terry left out to meet up with one of his friends I gathered as much of my belongings as I could. I didn't really know where I was headed, just knew I had to get out of there. I had two bags packed full of clothes and was working on the third when I heard a car out in front of the house. My heart sank with panic. Scurrying around grabbing whatever I could reach I finally made it to the door. Terry was coming in just as I reached for the knob. He immediately noticed something was wrong. Looking around he was able to piece it together.

"Where the fuck do you think you're going?" he spat.

"I—uh ..."

"It looks like you're trying to leave me. Is that what it is, Cook? You leaving me?" I was terrified. What could I say? Yes, and face his wrath? Or no and get caught in a blatant lie. I stood there in silence not knowing what to expect. We locked eyes for a split second then "Whack!" out of nowhere I felt the sting of his slap across my face. It had such force that it knocked me against the wall then to the floor. I reached up to my lip and tasted the blood that was trickling. Then I felt his weight mount onto me, his body reeking of alcohol, fists began pounding my face until I fell unconscious. I literally felt myself black out, then awaken...

"Ok, leave then." Wait. What just happened? I felt my face, my lip, no blood, no sting. He still stood there with fire in his eyes.

Maybe Momma was right, God was with me opening the door and allowing me to leave. I never looked back. My time with Terrence was an eye opener, realizing that being with an older man can run the risk of him taking you places you may not be ready for.

The groups of sports analysts were still debating when I passed them on my way to the bathroom. Inside was a row of ten sinks a half wall then about eight toilets lined up. There were no partitions, just butt-naked toilets. Like I said, no privacy; so, for the most part we're smelling each other's shit. Across from that were the urinals. At the back part of the bathroom was another half wall leading to the open showers, 5 heads on each side.

After I relieved myself, I returned to my living space or "cut," the area between the two beds that's divided by our lockers. As I gathered some things to start my day, I heard the noise escalating in the back of the dorm. Voices were rising which caused the tension to build. You can feel when something's in the air, it's best just to mind your own business like nothing is going on.

That kind of wisdom comes with time, unfortunately there are some young bucks that enjoy drama and rush to where it's at. Tempers were flaring to the point of no return and I knew where things were heading so I sat on my bunk and waited. Suddenly what I expected to happen happened. Evidentially someone said something that struck a nerve; the other someone got in their feelings and threw a punch and henceforth a fight.

"Get back! Get back! I want him one on one. He ain't workin' with nothin!" the aggressor yelled out after he shrugged off his weak punch. It turned out that the aggressive one was in one of the fiercest gangs on the compound. Lofton State Prison was well known for its violent offenders, a lot of stabbings and a couple of deaths had transpired in the past year. The events were enough to make the prison newsworthy.

Now the irony of the situation is if Jo-Jo, the non-affiliate beats up Clepto, the high-ranking gang member, he will have created a whole host of enemies. If he loses and does not give a good showing, then his reputation will be in jeopardy. Tough position for a civilian to be placed in. On the inside, you have to choose your battles wisely.

A rather large crowd formed in the back of the dorm where most of the battles go down. Anyone who could not see climbed up either on the top bunk or the division walls to get a better view. To me, this was a classic display of barbarism enjoyed by the masses like in those gladiator days.

The brawl engaged with Jo-Jo, the underdog, striking quickly, as he should've. He was smaller of the two but did have enough workout strength to fare well. Plus, he had better stamina than Clepto. Jo-Jo played all sports and ran the yard like a deer, Clepto, on the other hand, didn't do much in the sport department, unless you count hacking around in pick-up games. His forte was smoking plenty of marijuana and popping pills. He had certain white boys, who go to the pill-call window, on the payroll for their prescription medication. To him, that increased his high.

Jo-Jo's strategy was to keep the bigger Clepto at bay with a stiff jab while trying to avoid being grabbed by the burly opponent. It was working momentarily until Jo-Jo let his guard down and allowed Clepto to catch him across his left jaw. The shot stunned him and Clepto pounced at the opportunity to end it and really do some damage.

"Alright, homie, he's had enough," an outsider yelled out watching the blood spill out of Jo-Jo's mouth. Clepto didn't let up, he continued pounding his head on the concrete floor.

"Yo! Chill, bro, you trying to kill him," the voice came from one of his affiliates which seemed to snap him out of his enraged trance.

"12! 12! 12! Comin' in, they're comin' in!" People were scurrying everywhere as if they had a bunch of options to go elsewhere. The onlookers were what probably tipped the officers off that something was going on inside the pod.

The medical staff rushed to the scene after being called in when the officers saw all the blood. "Everybody! To your bunks, NOW!" the sergeant ordered in his authoritative baritone. "Shirts off, hands out in front!" this was their procedure whenever there was a fight, and they could not determine who the participants were. In this case we know one was in the fracas, they just carried him out on the stretcher. If any bruises on the hands or body were visible, then it could be presumed that you were in the fight.

When they got to Clepto, they didn't even ask any questions, just cuffed him up and led him out the dorm and on the long walk to the hole where he'd be locked in an isolated cell for who knows how long. And to think all of this started over a senseless argument about some guys who don't even know they exist. Just think, I haven't even started my day yet. This is the unpredictable life in the chain gang.

"That was crazy, right?" Preacher man commented as he took a seat at the foot of my bed. It was customary to get permission if you were a stranger but Preach comes to my cut at least once a day to see what's going on with me.

"Yeah, a little but I'm not surprised. Two buttheads? They were bound to clash."

"So, what you getting into today?"

"I've got to head to detail 1st movement. And after I get off, workout, shower, watch about a half of the Wizard's game then hit the rec."

"Man, you're so institutionalized."

"That's not true. I'm just in a routine, it helps with my time. Let me do me, man." I countered chuckling.

"Ok, fair enough. Well, what about tomorrow night? What you say we go up to church? They have a new group coming."

"You know I don't really do the church thing, Preach."

'C'mon man, I see you reading your Bible every morning."

"That's different."

"How so? When you read God's word, you're putting the church inside of you. Therefore, you are still "doing the church thing" as you say. Have you ever been up there?"

"Yeah, I went a couple of times last year. The service was just ok, nothing that really moved me."

"Then it's time for another shot. This group here is close personal friends of the chaplain."

"And how do you know that?"

"I heard it around. That's what they say anyway."

"They say, huh? They say a lot around here and it's usually wrong."

"The question is you willing to go and find out whether they're good or not? I even heard they're coming with their choir."

"If they said it, I guess it's official. Ok, you've convinced me."

"Adrian Upshaw, you've got mail. Bring your I.D." the officer called out from the front of the dorm. There were 1000 anxious bodies surrounding the young officer as he passed out the paper with their name on it.

When I got the envelope, I was shocked to see the return address. It was a letter from an old acquaintance of mine. We had agreed to fall back from being exclusive when I first got locked up years ago. I wondered what made Erika want to contact me after all this time.

Adrian,

I know you're probably surprised by me reaching out to you. Truth be told, I don't know what made me write you. Maybe it's because I miss you. I was listening to the radio the other day and heard a song that reminded me of you. The words that were written seem to be about you. I started thinking, wondering what if we never paused things? I could've been more supportive of you during your time away. Lord knows everyone needs someone in their corner.

It took me a minute to find you. I went online and found out where you were. Your mug shot doesn't look that bad, by the way, trying to look tough and all. Anyway, when I scrolled down on your M.D.C. file it showed me everything. Maryland Department of Corrections has a thorough and up to date database. By putting in your name it listed everyone with the same name, and then it broke down all the state's information for you.

What saddened me was the amount of time you've been away. Then I saw a glimpse of hope, you are coming home soon. So, if you need anything, maybe just someone to be by your side during this final leg of your journey, I'm here.

Erika

My first thought after reading Erika's letter was "REALLY?" She actually had the balls to sit down and put a pen to paper and send me some bullshit like that. We have not spoken in more years than I care to count, and she comes kicking this "I'm in your corner" foolishness. Who does she think she's playing with? My emotions are not to be tugged on. What kind of response was she expecting? I really decided to put us on pause because of how she was acting. Once she heard about my incarceration, it didn't take much to convince her that we should stay in the friend zone. After a couple of months of spotty conversation, I could sense her drifting. All of a sudden, she was busier than usual. Calls became less frequent on my end, mail slacked off and the one visit that we had even faded from my memory.

It wasn't really a hard decision to pull back; all the signs were showing me that moving forward would be best. At that period, I knew I had time to do, so doing it without the worries of a non-committed woman was a no brainer. Why she chose to write me now was beyond me.

After reading the letter once more, I felt it was due a response. Erika exposed her thoughts and I have some of my own that she needs to hear. Somehow, I believe she is being moved out of my life for a reason. "Say Preach, I think I'll take that offer for church."

CHAPTER 8
Cookie

MY THOUGHTS WERE ALL OVER THE PLACE AS WE traveled through the back roads of Northwest Maryland. The church van was semi-full with members who had been selected for the church's prison ministry. There were members of the choir, a couple of deacons, Sister Wilkins over the treasury, and me.

This was our first official trip inside Lofton State Prison. When we made the initial ride up here it was to get clearance to come in, meet with the warden and prison officials, get visitor badge pictures taken, and meet with the chaplain over worship services. We all had mixed emotions when we arrived. The unknown was a common denominator since none of us had done this type of ministering.

Tonight, the prison seemed to be more serene than in the daytime hours. Coming through the security check area we were routinely searched as most visitors were, metal detector, shoes off, no jewelry. I felt a bit violated but understood that this was just procedure. Some of the ladies in our crew were not that understanding, and a female guard had to step in when Sister Elliott caused a scene about the metal detector sensor going off every time, she was asked to go through it. It turned out that it was the metal underwire in her bra that was triggering the machine. She is a heavy breasted woman and had to retreat to a side room to show the cause of the disturbance.

The vibe inside the multipurpose room area was comfortable as we set up mics and equipment for our service. The room was not too big but wasn't too small either. There were rows of chairs, maybe enough to seat 200 or so, divided by an aisle. A podium was placed in front of the stage area where we were told the band and choir could congregate.

Once everything on our end was in order, we tuned up with a few songs. The choir director, Brother Thomas Chandler had us sounding good. He would signal the altos then the sopranos, finally the tenors to produce harmonies that blended to perfection. This was one of our strengths; we worked hard on our praise and worship. The word says it's a direct channel to summon the spirit. We wanted the spirit in the building for these men; it makes for a better service.

Carl chose to stay behind and allow me to head up this part of our ministry. I was surprised considering how much he likes to have his hands on things. Being in control makes him feel complete. This project was his brainchild, so best believe he was going to want a full report when we returned.

It was close to 6:30 in the evening, they had just concluded what the prison calls a census count, and the church crowds were flowing from the dormitories. I am sure they could hear the music on the outside because it was thumping through the speakers in here. The voices from our choir were angelic tonight.

"Let the Glory of the Lord, rise among us! Let the Glory of the Lord, rise among us! Let it Rise!" The guys in their starch white uniforms flooded in singing along with us. It was one big union and right at that point I realized that no matter where you're at, incarcerated or free, the spirit dwells. And you could see it in their faces that they were excited to see us and anticipating something magical happening.

From my position in the choir, I watched as the men continued to file in and remain standing while we performed another up-tempo praise song. Brother Chandler was conducting us and stepping to the rhythm like he was in the marching band at an HBCU. He was in rare form and the crowd seemed to feed off his energy. There was one guy who took to the aisle to perform his own dance which brought cheers from the audience. It was brought to an abrupt end when one of the guards approached him. He saw him and returned to his seat. That scene was a painful reminder of where we were.

We settled the music down and one of our deacons

stepped to the podium still filled with the spirit. He bounced in place and swayed from side to side.

"Yes, yes. The spirit is in here tonight!" he shouted. "Do you feel it? Is the spirit here? Did you bring it with you tonight?" he continued to shout causing many to raise their hands heavenward, shouting their hallelujahs. "Ok, let's settle down. We'll be doing this all night."

The keyboard player played something mellow as he began to speak. "I am Brother Isaac Glascow from Victory in Faith Baptist Church, and we are deeply honored to be here with you tonight. I brought some friends with me tonight. Do you like what you hear?" At that one, the keyboardist amped it up again then he brought it back down to a low tone.

"We didn't just come to entertain you; we have a word for you. We have testimonies for you. We have hope for you. And most of all, we have love for you. Can I hear an Amen?" There was a chorus of Amens pouring out from the crowd.

We took our seats, which were facing the inmate crowd. Brother Glasgow had them pumped up waiting on his next word. "Please stand to your feet in reverence for God and let us pray."

He gave a spine-tingling prayer, one filled with hope and inspiration, preparing them for what was to come. We've heard him give these prayers in service many times, so it was no surprise to see their reaction. It was time for youth ministers, Vaughn Powers to deliver the Word. The guys were in for a treat because Vaughn was an up-and-coming messenger for God. When he spoke, he evoked power.

He was not a big man in stature but had a way of projecting and coming off way larger than his appearance. "Let's give a warm welcome to Brother Vaughn Powers here to give you a word." They all stood and gave him a huge round of applause.

"Thank you, thank you. You can have your seats. I am so happy to be here tonight. This has been on my bucket list for some time now." His comment produced some laughter. "Y'all laugh but I'm dead serious. I've wanted to get into a facility and have an opportunity to deliver God's Word and to be an inspiration to you guys. I've been fortunate to avoid being where you are, but I have friends who weren't so lucky. My friends and I grew up in South East, Washington, D.C. I know all of you know how crime infested it was at one time. Our families were determined to protect us the best they could so we could make it out. I was fortunate enough to escape the hood without a single arrest, but some of my comrades didn't." It was quiet as a cotton rainstorm in there; the brother had their full attention.

"My message for you is that there is nothing impossible with God in your corner. The problems that you're facing, whether it's in the courts, family, health, or maybe just dealing with the separation from society, God has an answer for each one according to your situation. And guess what? He will answer every request; all you have to do is ask it of Him through prayer. You may not get the answer right when you want it, but I guarantee you will get it when you need it. His time is nothing like our time. We are an impatient generation, probably the cause of why a bunch of y'all are here now." You could see some stirring out there which meant that Brother Powers touched a nerve. It was good to see the connection between them. Ministering is a two-way street, it's just as much for the sender as for the receiver, that's the work of the Spirit. "If you have your Bibles, turn with me to Exodus 14:29, and let's discuss how Moses had to show his obedience and exercise his faith in God at the same time. Now, how many have heard of Moses?" There was a good showing of hands raised.

"For the most part you know of him delivering his people by crossing through the Red Sea with the waters parted while Pharaoh's army was in hot pursuit." Most nodded in agreement. "But what you probably didn't know was the journey before the miracle. Moses had to first convince a stubborn group of people that were content with being slaves. He had to make them believe in the unseen, believe that there was a better way of life somewhere else. He had to show them that there was a God who sent him to do great works. Moses was an ordinary man sent to do extraordinary things. The odds were heavily against Moses. There were many doubters. There were many who didn't want to leave their comfort zone for fear of the unknown. There were many who didn't believe Moses even after he showed them miraculous signs."

I could sense the buildup that was what made Brother Powers so gifted.

"I'm here to tell you today that you are the many. How many feel like the odds are against them?" Some stood to their feet. "How many feel like you're stuck in a place with no means of escape?" More rose to their feet. The spirit made me rise and Brother Power's voice became even more audible.

"Well, I'm here to tell you that there is a God that can do the impossible. When the water was in front of Moses, He told him to go, trust in me, and I'll part the water and you will walk to the other side on dry land. Believe in me, believe that I will do all that I say I can do. Who gave you speech when you couldn't speak? Who gave you power when you were powerless? Who gave you everything when you had nothing? That same God is at work today in each and every one of your situations. All you have to do is activate your faith. The Red Sea that needs to move is in your mind. God is telling you to trust in Him and just walk, let Him part the waters of your life so that you can cross over on dry land?"

Everyone was on their feet at the conclusion of his message. Brother Powers delivered as he does for us. It goes to show you that it doesn't matter about the building. Church is inside of you.

"Is there anyone out there who has a testimony to share? I think we have time for one."

A young-looking man stood and made his way down the aisle with the obvious astonishment of his peers. It was apparent that he was quite popular the way they shouted out what I assumed was his nickname. His uniform was immaculately pressed to the point it could probably stand on its own. He had a strong confident walk to go with his clean-cut appearance. I had to admit, he was very handsome, and had no shame in checking him out. I looked around there were a couple of other sisters whispering about the same thing I assume. Their guilt showed when I caught the starry eyed gazes, they gave him as he approached.

"Well praise God young man, what is your name and what do you have for us?"

"My name is Adrian Upshaw. I don't even know why I'm up here." That brought out a few chuckles. "Seriously, I don't even do the church thing, they can tell you." He pointed to a couple of guys in the crowd. "Your message was just so powerful and on point that I was moved to come forward. I have things going on in my life that need clearing up. Like you say, Red Seas that need to be parted. I guess I need to walk and let God do His thing." They shook hands.

"Well put Adrian. Can I ask you something, brother? Do you read the Bible?"

"I try to every morning."

"Then you do the church thing, bro. It's just not in this building. This place is made for fellowship with other brothers who believe. Iron sharpens iron, the more you're around those who you believe, the stronger you become. Your strength is shown by having the courage to come forward and express your weaknesses. For God says, in your weakness I will make you strong. Let's hear it for the strong and confident, Adrian

Upshaw." The crowd and everyone else rose to their feet once again and gave up a thunderous applause. It seemed to me that my claps were loudest of all. There was something about Adrian that touched me. I couldn't put my finger on it but whatever was going on, I wanted more of it.

CHAPTER 9

Cookie

"So, how did it go down at the prison last night?" Carl asked. We were still in the bed, he on his side, and me on mine. As a woman, I have needs, and last night was one of those times I wanted intimacy. My husband is who I'm supposed to go to in times of need.

I tried my best to create a mood by coming to bed in a lace negligee that I had bought hoping to spark some fire a few years back. We were fighting so much that pulling it out was the last thing on my mind, let alone lying down with him. After all, that had been going on, I still thought enough to make an attempt.

Having sex with Carl always seemed like a chore, like doing yard work, or mopping the floor or something. You put the effort in knowing what had to be done, but there was a lack of enjoyment. For me, that wasn't natural in a marriage that had struggled to last over the better part of 15 years. One of us had to step forward I would've expected for him to want to climb all over me since it's been so long, but that was hardly the case.

When I initiated at first his response was cold. Yet instead of pulling back, I literally forced myself upon him. I felt so desperate, never mind what my head was thinking, in between my legs was an uncontrollable throbbing that needed to be tended to. I took control, touching, kissing, and caressing him like he was my prince charming.

Closing my eyes took me to a different place, one that fulfilled my every fantasy. Passion had its way with me allowing me to lose control. Each movement had a purpose, each touch with intentions unsure. Heavy breathing overpowered me, making me labor for air. The contrast between pleasure and pain seemed to balance the scales. Inside of me there was a stirring of erotic energy that could not be contained any longer.

I allowed him to enter me, releasing vapors of ecstasy that had been trapped for quite some time. With his weight upon me, I let myself go receiving everything I felt I deserved. We produced a rhythmic motion causing him to whisper out obscenities in my ear. He went deep, I pressed back. He gripped me tightly and I submitted to his imposing will. When I clenched my fists into his soft skin, he came at me stronger.

His release came in a flood, waves crashing so hard those emotions could not be held back. My release was well overdue, and when I came the convulsions followed. We kept riding the moment, exploring a deeper realm of pleasure, something that had my mind spinning. With my eyes closed, all I could envision was my captor, the man who held me as a prisoner of love. This is what I hoped for; this is what I've been missing; this is what I want it to be like every time. This was my idea of lovemaking, something so unforgettable the man who is responsible never leaves your memory.

"Huh? Oh, it went well. The service was very inspiring. And Brother Powers preached a word that spoke volumes."

"He's good like that. I'm glad he is in the ministry; we need brothers like him to lead the youth. Now this is a bit off the subject, but how are you feeling?"

"I'm good, Carl, a little exhausted, why?"

"It's just you were quite animated last night, you know, when we were making love."

"I was?" He had me wondering what I did.

"Don't get me wrong, it was outstanding."

What's the problem? I mean, it's not like we go at it every night, or every weekend. Hell, every 3 months for that matter."

"Damn, you have to rub it in?" Carl's annoyance made him shift in defense.

"I'm just sayin."

"Well, since you're just saying, who's Adrian?"

"Excuse me?" What in the world was Carl talking about? He came out of left field with that one.

"You know what I'm talking about. You called out a name last night. Adrian. I heard it clear as a bell. I didn't say anything at first because I thought I was hearing things in the heat of passion, but then you said it again and again."

Oh my God. In all my years I've never had a moment like that. I was so embarrassed. How can you explain something like that? That's like the ultimate disrespect.

"Carl, I had no idea I was even speaking last night. I was moving off emotion. Don't really know what to say." He began to get out of bed and started to forcefully put his pants and shirt on.

"What's there to say? Nothing, I heard enough. Thanks for last night. I'm going over to the church. I'm gonna leave you to your thoughts."

And out the door he went. There was a deep pit in my stomach, a feeling of emptiness and it was not because I was starving. How could I have made that mistake? I rested there for a few more minutes, and then decided to start my day.

After I ate, I felt like I needed to talk things out with Maxine. Maybe she had some insight for why my hormones were on high. That had to be one of the causes for my mental error. Adrian. I merely watched the man say a few words so why did he have such an effect on me? Sure, he exuded a quiet confidence, but that was hardly enough to have a choke hold on my emotions.

I had to admit, on our way home from the prison, he did cross my mind. I wondered what he could have done to be in there. What was his life like before this? He appeared to have come from a decent background. You could just tell the ones who had it rough and he wasn't that type.

Anyway, the question is why was he on my mind in the heat of passion with my husband? Was it the lack of affection that I've been experiencing? Or maybe the intrigue of someone new was sparking an erotic fuse within me. Whatever the cause, I had to get control of myself before I do any more damage. It wasn't my intention to hurt Carl's feelings despite his recent actions. The phone chiming a familiar tune was a welcome distraction.

"Hello." I answered before looking at the screen seeing Carl's name. My mood instantly changed.

"Sandra, I can't help thinking that maybe there's something wrong with you."

"What are you talking about?"

"Are you still seeing that shrink?"

"Therapist and yes I am. I've been trying to get you to come with me, remember."

"Instead of trying to find problems in our marriage, you need to check with her about the voices in your head."

"Bye, Carl," I said before abruptly hanging up. How dare he accuse me of being sick in the head. True enough, I made a grave mistake, and he has a right to be upset but that shit was uncalled for. I think I'll give him some time to cool off. Even though today wasn't one of my scheduled days maybe calling Max and meeting with her is what I need.

I decided to take a ride downtown to one of my

favorite coffee shops to get a break from my hectic life. I turned onto I street and made my way a half block before finding a spot within walking distance of Chester's Coffee and Cappuccino. The short walk allowed me a chance to enjoy the fresh spring breeze.

I was seated in the patio overlooking the busy mid-morning traffic. I tried Maxine again after unsuccessfully getting an answer earlier. I still got the voicemail, so I left her a message. I knew she was not expecting me, but I was hoping that she had an opening.

Ironically, and what seemed totally coincidental, I looked down the street, a little across from me, and saw a woman who had an uncanny resemblance to Maxine. She wore dark shades, the big ones that cover your eyes and most of your face. I could see her look down at her phone as if she sensed me calling but didn't attempt to answer it. No, she definitely looked distracted.

A jet-black SUV pulled up alongside of her then stopped. She reluctantly walked up to the passenger side window, exchanged a few words with whoever was inside then reached in her shoulder bag and handed them a manila envelope. From my vantage point, it was hard to detect what was really going on or why she was having this type of secretive meeting. It just did not look right to me. The tinted vehicle drove off, leaving her standing there with a deflated posture. After looking around to see if she had been spotted, she exited into a nearby store. Then my phone suddenly rang, and I saw that it was her.

"Hey Cookie, I'm just now seeing your missed calls; I was tied up a bit."

I bet, I thought but didn't speak it.

"What's up?"

"I was trying to set up an appointment with you to talk."

"When? You already have one scheduled for later in the week."

"Today, if possible."

"That urgent?"

"I think so."

"Well, give me a few. I had my 2:30 cancel so I can give you that spot. Your timing is good." I wondered if she knew just how good my timing was when I stumbled up on her little meeting with the dark vehicle. "Give me an hour and you can meet me at my office."

"Sounds good." I closed the conversation and continued sipping my hot drink. Suddenly, Maxine appeared out of the store and walked to the corner where the SUV had pulled up on her before. What did Max have going on? Once again, she was looking around nervously. Then, as if she willed it, the same tinted truck screeched to a halt. Max jumped in, and then just like that, they vanished.

The whole scene was weird. One thing I wasn't going to do was question her about what I saw. Her business is her business. No need for me to jump to conclusions. I'd just keep an open eye on her actions and offer help when necessary. Besides, our friendship hasn't grown to the point where I could advise her on anything. She's still in the position of giving advice, and I'm paying for it by the hour.

I knew it would take some time to get out of the city traffic, so I settled in for the ride by turning into XM radio to lift my spirits. "Angel," by Lailah Hathaway was playing which took my mind away to a place unexpected. For some reason, my thoughts were drawn to the prison. Seeing all those men inside that room really made me think. There were fathers, brothers, sons, and nephews, even grandfathers, locked away from their families.

It was sad. The eyes I saw were void of life, lacking hope, only drab colors, and repetitive routines filled their days. The service we had was probably the brightest part of their week. You could see the pure joy in some of them, the way they danced, shouted, and praised God openly. I've heard so many stories about life behind the walls, but what I witnessed for myself was a genuine showing of love for the Lord, no different than in congregations in outside churches from state to state.

Really the only thing separating them from us is the barb wire fences we passed on the way in. That's why it was refreshing to see them in that element. It was like a free invite into the prison world. And they need love too, almost as much as air to breathe.

The one shining moment, besides the brothers who accepted Christ for the first time, was hearing Adrian Upshaw being honest about his faith and rededicating himself to his walk. That side of a man is as much attractive as it is admirable. It's kind of what drew me to Carl, what he had stored up inside made him unattractive to me.

My eyes did not wander in Adrian's direction by chance; there was a cause to that effect. From the beginning, I realized that Carl's love for me came with an agenda. Maybe it was to give him an offspring, our daughter Sharice, maybe it was a beautiful wife to make his First Lady, a show piece for the church, or someone to boost his self-esteem, overlook his insecurities and forever be loyal to his life's plans.

So now I'm kind of anxious for our next visit to Lofton State facility. I had an awakening; a new spark was lit inside. This was Carl's idea, his prison project. He wanted me to get involved in the ministry; well, I'm sure he didn't realize how involved I'd have to be in order to reach these men, Adrian in particular.

I arrived at Maxine's office with a new attitude. I was ready to share what's been going on in my world. To my surprise she met me in the parking lot. She must've showed up not too long before me.

"Cookie, I may need your ear today. There's some things I have to get off my chest that's been weighing heavily on me I know you wanted this session so today and your next appointment are on me."

"I'm here Max. Let's go talk."

CHAPTER 10

Adrian

GOING TO DETAIL EVERYDAY WAS PART OF MY ROUTINE that made my days go by. I report to the counseling area before the staff even arrives. They are due in by 8, I usually get in by 7:30. This all depends on whether the movement is on time. Anything could cause the delay in early morning traffic, from heavy fog to emergency counts; you learn to wake up to the unexpected.

Working in the counseling department is considered an administrative detail in prison and is looked at as a premier position. Being an orderly has its perks and downfalls. A lot of inmates covet such a detail because of the interaction with the staff, especially those in position to help. Counselors can get people in for visits, help get inmates into classes, but most of all they have influence on those who can help you get free. Of course, mostly women work in this area, which makes it a desirable spot to be in.

The downside to working there is people feel like you are the actual counselor and can move mountains. I constantly remind folks that I have absolutely no power and I wear the same uniform they do. They hear me but make requests anyway.

"I heard about you in church the other night. That was pretty brave to get up there and speak like that."

I was taken aback by her statement. Sweeping the floor was my only concern at the moment; I had just put a high gloss shine on it the day before and needed to maintain it. I was not expecting that comment from Ms. Breston. She was one of the counselors in the department.

"How did you find out about that?" I asked in astonishment. I really didn't think it was big news.

"Inmate.com," she said with a chuckle." "You know guys come in here, sit around and gossip while they wait on their appointments. Someone was talking about you when I walked by, so I tuned in." In my mind I wonder if guys have anything else to talk about besides each other.

"Wow, these guys around here are a trip. Even when you stay in your own lane, minding your own business, they still find a way to get in."

"In this case, it wasn't a bad thing. I didn't hear them tearing you down, at least not while I was standing there. It sounded like they were giving you props, like they had a new respect for you. Evidentially you have quite an effect on people."

The highlight that night for me wasn't what I did up at the podium; it was what I saw on my way up there. A woman sitting with the choir had caught my attention. I first noticed her when she was singing but got a much better look at her as I approached. I couldn't keep my eyes off her, breaking my trance purposely when I got close to the minister, as to not alarm anyone. In this environment everybody sees something and when they see it, they're compelled to tell somebody about it.

Since that experience at church, my mind has been preoccupied with coming up with ways to try and meet her.

"Hey! You over there mopping, did you hear anything I said?"

Truthfully, I don't recall when I actually tuned her out. My intentions weren't to be rude; I didn't even know she followed me to where I was working. "I'm sorry, Ms. Breston, my mind was somewhere else."

"Obviously. What has you so zoned?"

"Just trying to find a way out," I said it figuratively, but the statement had many connotations.

"A way out? Upshaw, your day is coming, you have to keep doing what you're doing, and things will work out for you." She meant well but was really saying what all counselors are trained to say to keep hope alive. I was working on forging another course of action. My idea of getting out there involved mind, body, and soul.

"I appreciate your words of encouragement, but do you know how many times I've heard those words over the 15 plus years I've been locked up? It just becomes a cliché after a while."

"Well, I didn't mean it like I was running lines on

you. I'm not your counselor, so I'm not in a position to give you information, good or bad, about your file. What I can tell you is that I've been keeping an eye on you," she disclosed to me from the threshold of her office doorway. Ironically, there was no one present in the hallway or the other offices. I believe she detected that as well, which prompted her to be a bit more forward with her actions.

"Upshaw," she called from inside her office, drawing me closer to hear her better. "If I were your counselor, I could do more, but since I'm not our counselor, I want to do more."

Ms. Pamela Breston was the youngest of all the counselors. Being in her early 30's, and having a degree in psychology, and being blessed with looks of a woman much younger than her years had her drawing the attention of inmates and haters amongst her peers. It was not her fault she was getting her life together while the other counselors were nearing middle age and enduring issues that had a couple of them seeing counselors themselves.

To me, Ms. Breston was the finest woman walking the compound here at Lofton, but because I worked in the department, I did not ever show that I saw her as beautiful in any way. People, well inmates in general, are quick to insinuate something whether it is true or false. I like where I work so I tried to keep a low profile to ward off attention.

Her approach took me by surprise, or maybe I was

blind to the attempts she is made in the past. Either way, she put it out there, which is the first step; it was up to me to move forward or not. I moved into the space in front of her desk. Leaning down, I spoke in a low tone.

"Ms. Breston, I would love for you to do more, but do you realize what you're getting into?" Her subtle flirting became more open in the comforts of her office. I guess she felt like she had control.

"Look, Adrian, I may not have been here long, but I'm no rookie working in prisons. I know the dos and don'ts. I watch how you move, and you keep the same demeanor every day, which is respected. It doesn't help that you're attractive, the other women in here see it just are afraid to act on it, but I'm not." Her boldness scared me yet turned me on at the same time.

What's the move?" I said bluntly. No need beating around the bush. She already put the ball in play. She stood reaching all of her 5'5, looked me in the eye with a stare that spoke a volume only she and I could hear. A door opening out in the hallway interrupted the next words from her lips. My prison instincts picked up on the keys jingling which alerted her. She reacted naturally, which showed me she was a pro.

"Ok, Mr. Upshaw, I'm gonna sign you up for my Change of Thinking class, and that should knock out your pre-release requirements." With a very professional posture, she shuffled some papers around, then watched as Mr. Brownlee, one of the older male counselors walked past, looking in briefly.

"Upshaw!" He called out in his gravely tone. At first, I thought he might have seen something that made him suspicious but ignored the notion. "Can you come shred some of these files when you get through in there?"

"Sure, sir, will be there in a sec." I looked at Ms. Breston to see if she was finished. "You good?"

"Yeah, I'm good. We'll get a chance to connect. Until then you already know where I stand, just stay cool."

"I got you."

"No, I got you," she said with a flirtatious wink.

The rest of the afternoon went smoothly. Ms. Breston left for a meeting, which took the pressure off, at least until the next day. I'll worry about tomorrow when it gets here. For the rest of the evening, I had to mull over these new decisions that had entered my life. The good thing about it was I had my own timetable to go by. I was more or less intrigued by both situations. The mystery woman had me anticipating the next visit from Victory in Faith. I didn't know if I would get an opportunity to say something to her or not, but my plan was to put myself in position.

Ms. Breston, on the other hand, had made things plain and clear. Her intention was to get closer, and just from the vibes she was giving off it was apparent her desire was to make things sexual. What I needed to do was to secure a means to communicate with her so we can keep our business off the radar. The eyes and ears of prison are forever lurking to catch some breaking news and I'll be damned if I'm on the front page of the Lofton State Gazette. Getting caught up in "personal dealings" as the administration calls it, is a one-way ticket to isolation/lockdown and more than likely a transfer to another facility to get you away from any other potential victims. For her, it could cost her the job, which is far worse than my punishment. Speculation alone can put blips on the radar, so I had to be very strategic.

When I got back to the dorm, all I wanted to do was to take a shower, eat a little something, and then relax. I wasn't in the mood for the dorm rats that do nothing all day but play dominoes, spades, checkers, or talk about people until the televisions come on, and then they find a way to argue about that.

"Man, I bet you Jay-Z and Beyonce have more money than Will and Jada Smith. I'm telling you bro; I know this for a fact." I heard while I showered.

"What makes you an expert?"

"Cause, P-Nut was on the phone with his cousin, who is from New York and does music. He be at the Grammy's and everything. Anyway, he said, his cousin said he was at this party with all these industry folks, and he overheard a conversation about bank accounts, they said the Carters were on top."

"That's all you got? Ice, those ain't no facts! I could get on the phone and find that out, in fact, that's all we gotta do. Google that, homie."

"Bet that, I'm a holla at Justo when he gets off the line and see about this."

"What you need to do is cop you a flop so you can call your cousin in New York and tell him to stop lying."

"Yo, get off my cousin, man. Hey Justo! I need to get one of them joints, holla at ya boy!"

After hearing that meaningless exchange, my wheels went to spinning. I wondered what Justo would charge to get me one of those phones. He keeps all his business private so I may have to send someone at him to get the information.

Preacher Man came over for his customary visit after I got myself together. I was hanging my wet towel up to dry when he sat at the foot of the bed.

"Hey man, what's good with you? Anything new and exciting happen at work today?" he asked. I would've looked at him strangely except that he asks the same question every day.

"Naw, nothing new," that was gonna be my answer from here on, gotta keep everyone thrown off. "Hey, Preach, you heard anything about Justo having some flops for sale?"

"I don't know if he's got them of if he's selling them for his partner. You know Glaze makes the moves and his cronies move the product. He's pretty smart about how he operates. I'll do some checking around and let you know."

"Please, I need something soon."

"Ok, but are you sure you want what comes with it? There's a lot of responsibility that goes along with having a cell phone. Instantly, you become the envy of all those who don't have one, not to mention always being on point, looking out for "12".

"Preach, I've got years under my belt," I responded confidently.

"Yeah, but this is a new age chain gang. These young boys don't have any understanding, and sure don't listen to the elders like when we first started doing time. They only live for the moment, never mind the day." Preach made a good point, he and I have both seen some of these young kids do some senseless acts, not worrying about the consequences.

There was a situation on the East side of the compound where one of the female officers was forced into a compromising position. A high-ranking gang member had found out that her nephew was an inmate in the dorm where they resided. He was a quiet guy, didn't bother anyone, just stayed in his room reading most of the day.

The dorm had about 20 different members of that gang which made life hard for civilians or non-affiliates. Corey was doing the right thing, stay out of traffic and you don't get hit by the car. He just had the unfortunate luck of having a relative who worked at the prison.

Officer Taylor was working the I unit when Zeus approached the control booth where she was doing her observations. He knew she had one more day on that post, so he wanted to make it count. Bending down to speak in the open area where she could hear, he gave her the ultimatum.

"Look here, bitch, we know you got your kinfolk in here with us, so this is the play. You gonna go out when you get off and bring us this." He handed her a piece of paper with a list of contraband items. "Have it when you come in tomorrow or we're gonna hurt your folks up really, really bad. You got it!" Her eyes nearly popped out of her head when she saw the serious look on his face. Fear froze her body, making the rest of her night uneasy.

She showed up at the building as planned the next afternoon and settled in. Maybe she went home, gathered her thoughts, and convinced herself that the young man was somehow bluffing. Well, it didn't take long to realize the naked truth.

To her surprise, she looked up to a horrifying image; Zeus was standing in front of her with Corey. He had his arm around Corey's neck in a choke hold.

"So, what's the deal, bitch? You got what I asked for or what?" He yelled now having everyone's attention. Her worst fears were before her, how could she get him out of this position? He was innocent in this whole ordeal.

"Please...please don't hurt him. I can get it. It will take some more time," she whimpered out.

"More time is what you don't have. You must've thought I was playing with your ass." Right then Zeus pulled out a 6' blade sharpened to a point. With her eyes widened she witnessed her nephew Corey get stabbed repeatedly to the neck, back and torso area. Blood squirted everywhere, even on the glass where she viewed the most graphic scene of violence in her life. It was too much to bear. She ran out of the control area and down the walk, all the way to the main entrance and through the door, never to be seen on the compound again.

Corey survived, but had major injuries that would take months to heal. The experience though, would affect him for a lifetime.

"Preach, I can handle myself."

"I hope so, bro. I hope so."

CHAPTER 11

Cookie

"I witnessed a crime," Max confessed.

"You what?" Now this was a role reversal, I was in her office listening to her issues. "When did this happen?"

"A few years back. This young man got convicted of murder because of my testimony. There's a chance for a retrial and the state wants to use me again as a witness."

"Ok...and?"

"Well, the boy I put away is in one of the major gangs here in the city and now they're after me to write a statement saying that I made a mistake in the identity."

"What are you going to do?" I was worried for her.

"I don't want to put a killer back on the streets."

"So, don't. Stick with your story."

"They threatened me and my son, Cookie. My life is on the line."

"Damn, Max. That's a tough choice."

"Not really, I already made it. I wrote the statement and gave it to them."

"How do you feel about it?"

"Scared to death. What if it doesn't do any good? These guys don't play by any rules."

"I know that's right."

"Don't think like that, he sent himself to prison by doing what he did. Besides, I think whoever you made your agreement with will honor his word and not harm you."

"Haven't you heard the old adage, 'There's no honor among thieves?' Well, I think that applies to thugs too."

"If you feel like you've done the right thing then leave it in God's hands."

"And if I didn't do the right thing, then what?"

"Still leave it in God's hands."

※

"Brother Powers, when the ministry goes back to Lofton State facility, I want Sister Andrews to bring the message."

"Pastor, have you run this by her yet? When we talked on our way back, she seemed content with her role in the choir. Plus, don't you think the message will better received by the guys if a man delivers it?"

"Brother Powers, you know the Word well enough to understand that we are mere vessels. If He could use a bush or a donkey to speak through, a woman, our helpmate can surely stand in the gap."

"You're absolutely right, Pastor Andrews. The spirit is definitely in that place. There are a lot of young brothers who appear to be ready to confess their sins and rededicate their lives. Peer pressure is their biggest obstacle. I saw all different types of men in that crowd dancing and shouting for the spirit. Men tatted from head to toe, homosexuals were there as well."

"Praise the Lord. The door is open to all."

"There was an older brother who stood the entire service. Danced, praised, read the word, and prayed standing. I was tired witnessing the energy he had." They both chuckled.

"Sounds like quite an experience."

"As a matter of fact, I look forward to our return."

"Good, because it should be sooner than you think. I spoke with the chaplain at the prison, and he made arrangements to up our visits to twice a month instead of once a month. He was pleased with the initial turnout, and we had a remarkable impact on the inmates and staff alike."

"Well, let's hope our team is as equally enthusiastic to make that trip."

"Oh, they should be. It's all in the name of the Lord."

Pastor Andrews was studying alone in his basement makeshift office. This was his mini sanctuary, the place where he retreats to and prepares his Sunday sermons. No one really comes down there without reason; his daughters knew that when he is in his office it's his time away. Cookie had learned long ago not to bother him with as much as a phone message from the church, which suited her just fine. This gave her some "me" time, and more time with the girls.

※

Chloe walked in the kitchen and saw Cookie and Reecie playing a board game. They looked like they were having so much fun that she didn't want to spoil their mood. She had been dealing with all sorts of issues at school; things that teenagers go through when having to make mature decisions.

The more popular girls were jealous of Chloe because of her budding relationship with Gabriel Meesures Measures. He is a high school basketball star with a promising career ahead of him. He just so happened to choose Chloe, a regular girl, living a regular life, and that bothers them. They seemed to think that she is undeserving of such a prize. Truth be told, they're just mad because he didn't choose any of them.

Another issue she was dealing with was the pressure being put on her by Game, Gabriel's nickname given to him for his basketball prowess. He has been increasingly persistent on having sex with her at the close of the season. The team was headed into the playoffs, so her time for deciding was running out. These things had been worrying her in such a way that it was affecting her around the house. It never crossed her mind to confide in someone who had been through her share of trials with men, her mother.

"Hey dear, you wanna join us?" Cookie asked, trying to include her in their fun.

"No thanks, I just came to get something to drink, and then I'm headed back to my room." She gave Reecie a half smile but avoided eye contact altogether with Cookie. What her mother did not know was that Chloe had discovered that she had been inside one of the hidden apps on her phone. Once the app was entered, it logs the time when you go back to make an entry. The time that displayed on the screen was when she was in school. Her mother had already said that she had been cleaning in her room while she was gone. For her, it was a huge invasion of privacy and she didn't know how to approach her about it.

"Is there something wrong, Chloe?" You've been cooped up in your room off and on for days. You know whatever it is we can talk about it, woman to woman."

"Really? Woman to woman, huh? How about telling me what business you have...oh, never mind, I'm out!" She jetted out of the room and went up the stairs before Cookie could put together what she was saying.

"Chloe!" She called out, but it was too late, she was out of earshot. There was nothing to be said without knowing what she was actually mad at her for. She decided to give her some time to cool down. What she was unaware of was Chloe harboring those feelings towards Gabriel. The more things became rocky at home, the more she sought out comfort in him. And with him being a senior, his maturity is what made her obedient to whatever his wishes were. In her eyes she saw forever, not to mention a way out. He could potentially be a huge star on the court and take her with him; that's a young girl's dream. But if it didn't pan out, it could be her worst nightmare.

❀

"I thought I told you not to contact me here. I'm at home you know." The person on the other end of the phone murmured something but Carl quickly countered. "No, it's not alright. I'll let you know when I'm available. Right now, I'm working, and I need my peace." They responded which softened Carl's mood a bit.

"No, no, you're good. I'm not trying to be rude or insensitive, just trying to concentrate on what I have going on here. I know you understand." They conceded with a halfhearted response.

"Well, you'll have to try harder because when I tell you something that's what I mean. I will contact you soon."

That seemed to satisfy them for the time being, but Carl knew that he had to get a grip on the situation before things got out of hand. Control was what he specialized in, so this was not going to turn into a problem, he was sure of it.

CHAPTER 12

Adrian

BIG BENZO CAME WALKING OUT OF MS. BRESTON'S office with a slouched posture. His walk was labored like he had the weight of the world on his broad shoulders. Counselor Breston had called him up to make a customary call home at his family's request. He was a big man, standing about 6'5, 240; however, whatever conversation he had on the phone minimized his size.

"It'll be ok, Bernard, she loves you and that's all that matters." Ms. Breston consoled.

"Upshaw, talk to your friend for me."

"Yes ma'am. What's up big dude?"

"Man, my momma called up here and told these folks my daughter has been asking about me. She said she wasn't going to eat until she spoke to me. You know I was on the yard when they called me. I thought somebody had died or something. Instead, I get here, and Ms. B put my little girl on the phone." The big guy started to break down when he spoke. "I didn't even recognize her voice, A.U. I've never even met my own daughter. I've been in this damn prison for 10 years, missing her growing up. My baby momma was pregnant when I caught this case and we ended up falling out so she wouldn't bring Imani to see me. Not one visit Adrian!" His voice boomed throughout the counseling area.

"Bernard, you gotta keep your voice down. There are other counselors in their offices." Ms. Breston alerted.

"My bad, Ms. B. Yo A.U., Imma head back to the dorm. I'll catch you in a few."

"Alright, man. Stay up. This is a start; things will work out."

"I hope so."

Seeing Benzo react like that made me realize that this place can bleed you of the things you are dear to. Emotions that are kept suppressed over time can come spilling out at unexpected moments. It's something you can't control, a human function that's born in the soul. In prison hiding your feelings is a learned behavior. An unnatural thing is so widely accepted in this environment, that's absurd to me.

I wound the cord up and around the floor buffer, getting my supplies together to close my day. The counselors had emptied out of the conference room after their days end meeting. Everyone except counselor Breston had clocked out and headed home. Today was her last day, all the counseling staff had a designated day to finish paperwork, field calls, or deal with their cases. Benzo was on her caseload.

I didn't think I was in the mop closet that long. Things were in such disarray in there. I had to reposition some items just to get the buffer back in. The knock on the door startled me. No one ever tries to come in here, hell I didn't even like being in there.

"Adrian, what are you doing in there? I was out here calling you." It was Pamela peeking her pretty face in the doorway. She had one of those short hairstyles that resembled Megan Good in "Think Like A Man..." Skin was flawless, smile was radiant, almost angelic to the sight, yet she was staring at me with desire in her eyes.

"I'm sorry, I didn't hear you. Did you want something?" I asked, finally turning towards her.

"Um huh..." she bit her bottom lip in the most seductive way. "You." Right then she closed the space between us and reached for my face. I guided her hands with mine and led my lips to hers. We both completely forgot that we were in the mop closet, not to mention I was an inmate engaging in a heated kissing session with a staff member. This was supposed to be off limits and the epitome of crossing the line. However, our passion had overtaken our ability to think in the moment. I pulled away momentarily. She sensed my apprehension and calmed my thoughts.

"Relax; I've locked the outside doors." She had all this planned out without my knowledge. How did I miss all the signs? She pulled me back into her kiss, this time our bodies molded together so closely. I could feel her heart beating. Her hands probed over my shoulders, down my back, then gripping my ass through my pants.

That made me kiss her harder, not believing that she was that forward.

This prompted me to explore her body, something I haven't done to a woman in more years than I care to mention. The feeling was almost lost, but quickly regained with a touch on her breast. I could feel her nipple grow to hardness through the satin soft material of her blouse. The buttons opened easily with the flick of my fingers, revealing her ample cleavage escaping out of the lace clad bra.

Her heat radiated the small space we were in, her soft moans were like a secret language spoken, and telling me that she was enjoying what was taking place. Undressing her had to be controlled. I didn't want to seem too anxious, considering the element of time as well. She assisted me in the process by unlatching her bra and sliding the straps over her shoulders allowing her round breasts to fall into place. Instantly I was awakened down below and because we were meshed together, she could feel it too. I didn't mind and surely wasn't embarrassed. I was doing what most men in here could only fantasize about.

Pamela lifted my shirt over my head then quickly went for my belt. I, in turn, took the lead and removed my pants and boxers, standing there with my manhood facing north. As if on cue, she inched her skirt up and slid her thong panties down far enough to receive me comfortably. Under normal circumstances I would have been concerned about protecting myself, but this situation was far from normal. Any other thought besides taking her would probably compromise my position completely.

"Oh yes.... yes. Just like that. Put me up against the wall, Adrian. Fuck me like I'm a bad girl!" The things she was whispering in my ear was turning me on. It made me forget where I was and who I was doing it to.

Her breathing became more intense as we increased our pace. I was stroking her aggressively while holding her arms above her head, pinning her body against the wall as she desired. Then, turning her around, I made her face the door and entered her from behind.

"That's what I'm talking about," she screeched out. As she pushed back, I caught her rhythm and returned it with my own force.

The deeper I went, the harder she bucked. My senses were returning back to where I was, not wanting to get lost in the moment and get caught in the act. In prison, being on point in every situation can save you from trouble. This was one of those times when I had to steer things in a safer direction. I decided that ending this episode would be best, or there might not be another one.

I picked up my pace which excited her. For me, the aim was to ensure that I come, preferably not inside of her. I brought her to the brink of climax by reaching around and playing with her clit. I wasn't so far gone that I didn't remember what gave a woman pleasure. She fell back against me, weakened by my simultaneous stroking. I felt her release through my fingers, making me want to erupt.

Pamela smiled through heavy pants of breath. Her chest still heavy trying to draw in air in that small area we chose to make our sex clubhouse. We both gathered our belongings, and ourselves not knowing what to say or where this would put us in the grand scheme of things.

"Uh...I guess I should clean up this mess," I said breaking the uncomfortable silence.

"Yeah, I think so. I'll be in my office when you get through."

Like a kid who had his hand in the cookie jar, I wanted to get away before I got caught with the goodies. After finishing in the closet, I gave Ms. Breston a half-hearted wave before exiting the office for the day. I guess she already knew the move because the door was already unlocked for my departure. There was no need for pillow talk, or a recap for that matter, we had to see each other in the morning. Who knows what kind of vibe would be in the air with a full assembly of bodies around? Sleeping on this experience was going to be enough. I'll worry about that challenge first.

Preacher Man had some news for me the following day after I returned from work. It was a welcome distraction to the day I was having. Working around a woman you just had unauthorized sex with wasn't an easy task. For some reason I felt like everyone was watching me, like they watched our sex tape on one of those porn sites. She was in rare form, acting normal; like that mop closet wasn't just a seedy motel room not even 24 hours prior.

"Hey bro, I found out what the ticket is on those flips Justo pushing."

"Cool. What they talkin' bout?"

"$350 for the standard flips, you know them throw away joints we had on the street years ago."

"Damn, them joints only cost like $20 bucks at the dollar store, right?"

"Something like that. Anyway, if you want the upgrade, the smarts go for $550 or $600.

"For real, man? That's highway robbery."

"Yeah, they're making a killing. They know brothers trying to get out there. If you want to play, you gotta pay, I guess. Justo and his boys got the game messed up. They're going fast so you want me to get him to hold one for you?" My mind was racing trying to figure out how I was gonna pull together that kind of cash. Even at $350 that wasn't just something you could tell someone to send you without questions. Then when you tell them a cell phone, that's where you get the third degree, at least that's how my family rolls. I'm going to have to go another route. I'll figure it out somehow."

"Yeah, tell him I want one of the flips."

CHAPTER 13
Cookie

I LOOKED AROUND WATCHING PEOPLE ENTER THE church and noticed that it had turned into more of a fashion show than a place of worship. Sister Williams in her big floral hat dressed to the extreme, making sure every detail matched. Her teenage daughter followed in her footsteps wearing Louis Vuitton and a form fitting dress, like the club was her next destination.

Even the men were partaking in the festivities. Brother Roger Brown, a regular member, had on his Sunday best. Known for being a dapper dresser, his only competition was himself. Sporting a pinstriped Brooke Brothers tailored suit, matching tie and pocket square, everything navy blue, the color of power.

I kept my eyes focused on the entrance waiting for Chloe to arrive. I tried to push her to get up and get ready for church. Reecie even attempted to wake her but she shooed her away, insisting on more sleep. If we waited on her, we would have been late. She assured us she would be there, saying that she would catch a ride with Ramona, another girl her age. Her parents were members and stayed in our neighborhood Ramona was privileged to have her license and a car. Being an only child had its benefits and Chloe seemed to be a beneficiary.

This was an especially important morning for her to be in service, Reecie was doing her first solo dance which she had been practicing for months. Her hopes were for her big sister to be there. She wanted desperately to make her proud. Lately I have seen more of an effort from Chloe to be a part of Reecie's life. Even if she and I weren't the closest, I want there to be harmony between the girls. It doesn't matter that they don't share the same blood; they share the same roof which makes them sisters in my book.

In came Chloe. The doors creaked open then closed alerting everyone that someone had entered. It caused a bit of a stir within the congregation before they turned their attention back to stage where Reecie was performing. She tried her best to concentrate on her movements but stumbled on a difficult maneuver. She recovered quickly and finished gracefully; however, you could tell she was disappointed in herself, even more so at her sister.

"Why were you so late?" I asked as Chloe scooted in next to me on the pew.

"We got tied up. I tried to get here. Reecie did great," she said, trying to divert Cookie's attention. What she didn't want to reveal was the real reason that she was late.

"Where's Ramona? Her mother has been looking for her too."

"Uh.... she just dropped me off, but wasn't coming in." Truth was she never caught up with Ramona. Gabriel was the one who brought her to the church, after taking her to breakfast. Chloe made a call to him as soon as she heard her mother and Reecie pull off. As usual, Carl had to be at the church bright and early to get things organized for Sunday school. That allowed her freedom to use extra time to her advantage.

She enjoyed her time with Game, almost too much. They lost track of time, which put her in panic mode to get to the church. Game did everything in his power to reach her destination, even avoiding the lurking speed traps set by the police. It was to no avail.

"Now that's strange, Sylvia got a call from Ramona, before your father's message, she said Ramona was suffering from cramps and had been bedridden since sun rise. So, what's really going on? And please don't tell another lie up in here. I couldn't stand for lightning to strike us both."

Chloe was speechless. Her mother was on to her. How did she think she would outthink her mother who had been through much more in her lifetime, and plenty of liars, too many to count? "We'll discuss this later. I

don't wish to ruin Reecie's day." Just then Sherice moved into the pew looking to be consoled. "You did really good honey!" Her eyes brightened.
"Did you like it Chloe?"
"Amazing! Encore, encore!" Reecie smile broadened.

I just rolled my eyes knowing I had my hands full with Chloe. She was testing my patience as a mother, something I was hoping not to repeat with Reecie.
"When were you going to tell me that I'd be preaching at the prison?" I was fuming after I heard the news from Brother Powers. He came to me when service concluded. We always have a post service meeting to review issues, so I thought I would address my gripes. At least I had the decency to do it in private.
"Sandra, hold your voice down," Carl countered in a stern tone. "I only did that because I feel you are ready. Why not there?"
"Ah...maybe because they're criminals. I wouldn't know what to say to encourage those men. What kind of impact could I have?"
"I believe a huge one, sweetheart. I've heard you before, remember, you're a gifted speaker, one that the men need to hear. It doesn't matter who delivers the message, it's the message that's important."
It's been a long time since Carl has actually said something supportive to me. I felt a little better knowing that he believes in me I just pray that the guys believe in me too.

"On another note, I really think you need to talk to your daughter."

"What? I thought Reecie performed well."

"Not Reecie, Chloe. She is getting to be a handful, more than I can handle myself."

"Last I recall, we were both parenting in this situation."

"Well, lately she's been doing her own thing, excluding herself from family activities, talking back, and most recently lying.

"She's a teenager, Sandra, those are normal things they do at that age," he said nonchalantly.

"See there you go defending her actions again. This is serious, Carl. Her lying is leading me to not trust her. I don't want her behavior to be an influence on Reecie. You know how much she admires Chloe.

"And that's good, younger siblings are supposed to emulate their older ones."

"There are good and bad influences. What if Chloe was smoking crack? Would that be something you'd want Reecie to copy?"

"Is that what you're trying to tell me? Chloe is sneaking off, smoking crack." Carl joked with a sarcastic tone.

"I was making a point. Oh, never mind. Just talk to her. As her father you should know what's going on in her life. Everything isn't all about church; we have issues in our household that need to be tended to."

"What are you implying? I provide very well for the household, thank you," he said in defense.

"Well how much do you know about what goes on inside of it? It requires more than monetary contributions to be head of a family. The way you manage the business of the church, just put forth a portion of that effort at home and I'll be happy."

"You'll be happy? I thought this was about kids?"

"It is Carl. If they're happy then I'm happy. Chloe needs help, I need your help, I'm doing all I can."

"I'll talk to her."

※

Maxine received a call from an attorney representing Richard Crawford. He stated that the statement that she submitted was inadequate and that she needed to present something a little more detailed. It was either that or refund the cash contribution that was given to her by Richard's associates. Maxine's heart sunk, knowing that paying back $50,000 was not an option. The money had been long gone; she should have known that money came with strings attached. She was sure that they would not be understanding when they came to collect.

"Cookie, what should I do?" Max asked her new friend after sharing the news of the call. She had reached out to Cookie and requested that she meet her for a late lunch at a secluded restaurant out in Greenbelt.

"This is an even bigger hole than you were in before. The whole situation seems messy, I don't know."

"To me, it seems kinda fishy. How do I know how

much or how little to write in a statement? Maybe they should coach me on what to say, that's the only way to give them what they want."

"What they want is for you to tell what you saw, only exclude any details that incriminate their client."

"In other words, lie through my teeth."

"Exactly. Not unless you have 50 grand stashed somewhere." I joked.

"I wish I did."

"There's no telling whether that would keep them from coming for you."

"Well thank you for making me feel better about the situation. I was better off calling Stephen King to come cheer me up." We both laughed, needing humor to segue the mood.

"For real, girl, it's a catch 22, because if you actually give a detailed statement it will undoubtedly keep long him imprisoned for a long time. Now, on the other hand, producing a false statement brings you at risk of getting yourself locked up. What if they have a retrial and you're asked to take the stand, finding out that you've falsified your testimony would be considered perjury." Silence commanded the moment.

"I need some time to really think about what I'm going to do. I have no direction, and to be totally honest, I'm scared. I almost wish I never saw what I saw."

"But you did, so let's not dwell on that. How much time did the lawyer say you had?"

"He didn't give an exact timetable, all he said was soon."

"We'll figure something out."

"Thank you, friend."

"Don't thank me yet, let's get you out of this jam first."

CHAPTER 14

Adrian

I LOOKED UP AND WONDERED WHY EVERYONE WAS surrounding the entrance door to the dorm. My curiosity led me to the crowd to see what the commotion was about, then I saw the traffic in the sally port. The only things that draw this type of attention from the men were some women in the vicinity, new arrivals to the dorms or a fight.

If there were women present you would hear the usual catcalling from the high testosterone brothers who could not control themselves and want to blame it on the years accumulated without female interaction. The truth was easily hidden behind an excuse, when admitting you have a lust problem reveals another problem, pride makes denying it so easy.

Today there were guys lugging large bundles containing all their property lined up waiting for their new dorm assignments. These guys were recognizable, which meant that they were getting released from isolation, or "the hole." Some looked as if they had been forgotten by the way their hair and beards had grown out. Once they were given directions, they collected their belongings and mattresses and entered their respective dorms.

We only had two beds open so we were anxious to see who would inhabit our dwelling. Actually, guys were more interested than me, some people are really caught up with controlling who lives around them. It was an unwritten rule that if you didn't fit the culture of the dorm, there was a good chance you could be turned around at the door by the authoritative figures in the dorm. If it is revealed over time then the same results could occur, being asked to exit the dorm, willingly or by force.

Two totally different guys came through the door. One was a scrawny white dude, hair disheveled, looking uneasy about his surroundings. When he opened his mouth to speak to some of the guys in his section, the bottom row of his teeth was chipped, blackened, and some missing, a classic example of drug abuse. His drug of choice was most likely methamphetamines judging by the aftereffects. We will see how long he lasts before he borrowed some money and cashed out.

The other inmate who came in was more well known. In fact, a lot of his homies showed up like baggage handlers at a hotel to carry his property and mattress to his bunk. Richie Rich stayed back to greet a few of his basketball buddies who gave him a warm welcome. He had a storied journey at Lofton State Prison. From his athletic accomplishments that still had the administration talking to his disciplinary issues of late, which has also been a major topic of conversation. Many thought with the lengthy time he spent in the hole, his next destination would be another facility.

His belongings were placed on the top bunk across from mine. Everyone in our section went over to greet him and to catch him up on the latest happenings since he has been off the compound for months. Although not much has really gone on, his violent act on the other side, causing that officer to quit, was the biggest news in a while.

Even Preacher Man exchanged a few words with Rich when the others left. Seeing them together was like watching an odd couple, two totally opposite personalities. One highly ranked and respected gang leader, and the other a devoted man of faith dedicated to changing his path. They do have something in common. They are consistent in the way they live.

I overheard bits and pieces of their conversation. "Man, they tried to case me up over that situation. Internal affairs came down here to talk to me and everything. They were more on the institution than anything, ready to launch an investigation on inmate safety. I'm glad it's kinda blown over some, I'm trying to get back in court."

"How's that coming along?" Preach inquired.

"I got my lawyer handling things. I got a letter from

him in the hole. He said he talked to the bitch who sent me here."

"I thought your co-defendants got you jammed up?"

"Yeah, they did some bone headed shit, but this broad had witnessed the lick we were on."

"Do you know who she is?"

"No. He says she's some shrink, listening to people's problems and shit. I had my boys pay her a visit and give her a little cash to change her statement. It turns out that all the other evidence is circumstantial; her statement is what's holding me. I swear I'll have that bitch touched up real nice if she don't switch her story up."

After hearing Rich recount what had happened between him and that woman, it really made me think about how people will see things going on, but they have a choice whether to report it or not. That choice comes with consequences either way, now this woman is faced with the consequences of her actions. I'm sure if she could choose again, she would live life like we do in here, see but don't see.

Anyway, I had way more on my plate to focus on, primarily the things going on at my detail. Every day was strategic now, watching who's watching me; making sure I'm staying consistent with my movements, not to raise any suspicions. Pam, on the other hand, was a natural, acting professional and flirty at the same time. I still had to keep a firm grip on the wheel to make sure we didn't crash.

To keep our conversations to a minimum in the office, I had to come up with another way for us to communicate. I had to get a phone. At first, when Preach quoted me the price for the phones, I thought it would be a major obstacle to get the money. Then I came up with a plan.

"Preach, did you tell Justo to hold that flip for me?" I asked my partner as he sat down in his usual spot at the foot of the bed.

"I did, but I don't know how far my word will go. You know how he is about the money, first come, first serve. I saw Richie Rich over there talking to him a minute ago, he keeps money on deck, so I'm pretty sure that he's lining something up."

"Ok," was all I said. I had a plan A, but I might have to activate plan B just in case.

There was another way I can get something in motion, but I would have to put in some work and have a couple of things go in my favor. First things first, I need to see where Ms. Breston's head is at, besides in my pants If she's interested in helping me out, then we're on the same page. If not, then we're headed down a road to nowhere. Being someone's chain gang boyfriend is not part of my immediate plans.

I reported to work like normal the next morning, but with a new attitude. My mood was up, very personable with all the counselors in the office. I kept everything cordial with Ms. Breston, waiting for the right opportunity to have our conversation. With all the various movement, I could not find the proper time.

"Why you look so stressed? I've been noticing you uptight all day."

"Just thinking about some things. I need to talk to you, but the timing hasn't been right."

"We'll have some time in a few. Everyone has classes to teach, and Chief has a meeting with the Warden. I hope it's not bad." She gave me the puppy dog eyes as she passed by me. Pam was looking exceptionally good today, making it hard to concentrate on work or anything for that matter.

Her hair was hooked up like she was fresh out of the salon and her pantsuit fit her well. With her stylish eyewear and sexy walk, she came off more like a seductive librarian than a prison counselor. As much as I wanted to grab her up and take her back into the closet where we first made love, I had to maintain my composure for both of our security.

"I'm good. I'll be over here working. Holla at me when you're free."

After another hour or so of spot work on the floor, filing here and there for the staff, taking out the trash, and filling up ice coolers, I finally had a chance to take a breather. I was so consumed in my tasks I didn't notice the remaining inmates and few counselors depart, leaving Ms. Breston in her office with the door ajar. When I peeked in, she was on a conference call but held up one finger telling me to wait a moment for her to finish. I stepped out only to see her end the call abruptly.

"Adrian!" she called out, using my first name like we were college sweethearts.

"Yes, ma'am," I said professionally, trying to hide my smile.

"Go 'head on with all that. What's on your mind?"

"Pam, I need help." I got right to the point.

"I'm here for you, to do what I can." I heard the sincerity in her voice, so I proceeded.

"Well, I want to talk to you more than just up here."

"So, we need to get you a phone, is that what you're getting at?"

"Ah…yeah. You cool with that? I mean, it will keep the eyes off us up here. We can act natural, hell, some days I may not say a thing to you."

"I wish you would start actin' stank like that."

"Ok, ok, I'll speak from time to time."

"No, you keep yourself like you been doing." She had an attitude in her voice which I thought was cute. She was catching feelings on the low.

"So how you wanna do this?"

"Well, you know security is tight around here. It's probably easier to get a gun in here than to get a cell phone in."

"For real?"

"Just kidding on that, but it is airtight. What they selling for in here? $300, $400?"

"How do you know all that?"

"C'mon, I keep my ear to the street. Besides, you know these folks talk around here."

"Yeah, a little too much obviously. The last I heard they were on the market for $350, that's for the flips, $500 for the smarts."

"Smarts?"

"Oh, my bad...smart phones, touch screens."

"Damn, for real? That much? Man, they're getting over."

"They got us by the balls because if we wanna talk we gotta pay."

"We'll have to make a way for you to get straight."

"What you thinking about?"

"Just keep doing what you're doing. Don't worry so much. I don't want you walking around here like you were today."

"Okay, momma."

"I got your momma, boy," her shy smile was infectious. I returned her gesture before I left to get back to the dorm.

When I got in, Preach hit me with the news that Justo had sold all the phones he had. The last one went to Richie Rich. I was a little disappointed. Even if I had the money, the phones were not available. From what I hear, it would be a few weeks before things picked up on the black market.

The next morning things started slow due to heavy fog. Movement is always halted when the visibility is minimal, like someone would be brave enough to scale four 10' high fences covered with razor wire on both sides. If they did succeed, by the largest of miracles, the amount of blood loss would eventually kill them. I'd sure like to hear a story from an escapee, but I won't hear one, because there hasn't been a record of any.

Pam and I met eyes when I finally made it to the

detail. She appeared to be glad to see me. Her brief glance was enough to let me know she was thinking about me. I put my coat up and began my morning routine of collecting the trash from all the offices. When I got to hers, she barely peered up from a folder she was engrossed in.

"Upshaw, you may want to check the closet, I heard something like a bottle burst in there. Did you have some chemicals stored overnight?"

"I don't think so," I said now wondering what I could have done wrong. Then she mouthed the word "GO!" Without a second thought I scrambled to the closet trash bag in tow. I looked around inside and did notice some bottles, but none were punctured. In fact, all were empty. But what I did see was something that looked out of place. Under the lip of the sink there appeared to be some fresh tape, it definitely wasn't there the day before. I reached my hand underneath to see what was taped there I was filled with joy. To my surprise there was a brand new, top of the line, smart phone was in my hand!

"How did she?" I didn't even want to ask; I was just thankful. Instantly, I had to train my thoughts back to prison mode. "How was I gonna hide it for the rest of the day?" How am I gonna get it back to the dorm, past the metal detectors?" Where am I gonna put it once I get it there?" I never considered these issues because, truthfully, I didn't think I would actually have one, not this exclusive anyway. I'll deal with it one step at a time, first I need to thank Pam for pulling this off.

She was outside her office when I came out with the

buffer. She looked around then winked at me when no one was looking.

"Hey, tell Chief I have to run this buffer to the shop to get looked at, it's been acting up."

"That sounds like a plan," she said totally understanding my ploy I had the phone taped underneath and with all the metal on the buffer, the gate officer would be foolish to stop me when the machine goes off. I'll take care of the rest when I get to the dorm. I was just so amazed at how she managed to do the impossible. I guess I underestimated her, but I'll never make that mistake again!

CHAPTER 15

Cookie

"I'M GOING TO PRAY FOR YOU, SISTER." I VOICED openly as I watched the bailiff clamp the handcuffs on Maxine's slender wrists. It was enough to see her squirm on the stand while the prosecutor hit her with a barrage of questions about her witness statement. I came for moral support. But at the conclusion, I was not at all expecting those results and it was me that needed consoling. Maxine and I had developed a friendship which extended past the office, beyond payment and advice. We became more to each other than doctor and patient, there was a connection.

When the presiding judge found her in violation of the constitution by perjuring herself under oath, my worst fear was confirmed. Her newer version of her statement was stricken from the record after it was read and compared to the original. Never in her wildest dreams did she think she would be in this position at this stage in her life. All her professionalism and degrees could not elude her from this jam she's in.

Ironically, Richard Crawford still had to find a defense. He had been transported back to Prince George's County where his crime was committed. After meeting with his legal team, they were in agreement with allowing in Maxine Stinson to testify for him as their witness. She alleged that there may have been some discrepancies in the details she claimed to have seen.

It went South when Max stumbled over her words, appearing to be a lot less confident than when she first took the stand. The legal team knew they were in trouble because they were well aware of the capabilities of prosecutor James Unger. He had a legendary way of making witnesses squirm, and it was his mission to make sure the infamous Richie Rich stayed in prison. If not for this offense, then for the other crimes he had on his record.

Now he is left to produce some sort of newly discovered evidence to convince the courts to either lessen his sentence or overturn the conviction altogether. Meanwhile, Max must face the harsh reality of county jail time, at least for a few nights. I plan to do whatever it is in my power to bond her out. I cannot let her stay in that place any longer than she needs to.

"Carl, I need some money," I stated flatly after racking my brain trying to come up with a solution. It was the last thing on earth I could imagine doing, asking Carl for anything especially helping me help a friend. My friend wasn't his so that alone lessened the importance. Then, the fact that it was Maxine Stinson, "the shrink" as he called her, didn't make it any better. In his mind he probably thought she deserved whatever punishment she received.

He just chuckled to himself. "Ok, humor me, exactly what is it that you need money for?"

"If I told you, you wouldn't want to help me."

"Try me. What you wanna do, shop? No, it can't be that I've been buying most of your clothes lately."

"Unfortunately, but that's not it. Are you gonna help me or not?

"How much are we talking about?"

"Oh, never mind."

"See, I knew it was something crazy."

"Crazy of me to ask," I said low enough for me to hear.

"Huh?"

"Nothing, I'll figure it out."

Our choir director was in full swing at rehearsal this afternoon. I had to admit we were bringing the noise, thanks to his anointing. Millicent Scott sang a solo that resonated all the way to the heavens. With us joining in to back her up, the song was truly our voices speaking to God. For her to be only 25, she had pipes way beyond her years.

"Sister Allen, you're over the treasury department, aren't you?" Everyone was gathering their belongings preparing for departure when the idea hit me.

"Yes, there's a group of us, but I head it up. Why do

you ask? Did something not figure right with my monthly reports? Please don't tell Pastor Andrews."

"Whoa, slow down, Sister Allen, I'm not here to dime you out to my husband. I have my reasons for inquiring. I'll be in touch."

"Ok, ok. Cool, just let me know what you need."

"I intend to."

I got lost in my own thoughts on my ride home. So many complexities were filtering in and out that I didn't know which one to focus on first. Between my issues at home with Chloe and Carl, and Maxine's looming situation, which has vaulted to the front of my mind, exactly where I did not want it now. I started to think about what kind of message I could take with me to the prison. The scheduled trip was approaching sooner than I had expected.

With the thought of the prison, Adrian automatically came to mind. I wondered what he was doing. How did he spend his days? His world was so foreign to mine, yet I'm sure there are some similarities too I can imagine a conversation with him would be interesting. There would be so much to learn about their environment. That could give me a better perspective of how they live, and what their spiritual needs are. I will be in a better position to serve them.

My slight daydream almost made me crash into the car in front of me. Evidently, they had been stopped at a red light, and if I had not jammed on the breaks, I was surely going to cause a heap of damage to their car and mine. I couldn't even think of how I would explain that.

Maybe that was a sign telling me to concentrate on what was in front of me.

I saw my gas light flashing and I realized that my attention had been on other things, rather than the important things, such as making sure I got home. The nearest station was not far, but it wasn't in the best area to be stopping, especially for a woman after dark. To go any further, to another station would be risky, so I would take my chances, get in and out, then take my behind home.

This was against all my morals and principles, because under normal circumstances I would not be out alone, outside in the dark, pumping gas. That is why I paid only enough to get me home and started for tomorrow. So, it wouldn't take me long. That was the plan any way.

A black four door sedan with tinted windows screeched to a halt right in front of the entrance. It caught my attention when all four doors including the driver's side and everyone masked, dressed in all black ran into the store. I heard a couple of shots, which was my cue to jump in my car and hightail it out of there. It only took a split second to remember what had happened to Maxine. I decided it was best to get as far away from that scene as possible so that they could not say that I saw anything.

On my reminiscing ride home, I wondered how many crimes like that occur that are witnessed but not reported. Witness statements have convicted so many criminals. The police investigation is made easier because of the outside assistance. I'm sure if something were happening to me, I would want an eyewitness, so it just depends on what side of the fence you're on.

"Where have you been? There has been someone from the county jail calling every five minutes." My thoughts immediately went to Maxine. Was she alright? Did she need something? Of course, she did her freedom. "See here comes another call, this time you answer it."

"Yes, I'll accept," I said in the receiver after the operator's recording announced there was a collect caller. "Are you ok?"

"Yeah girl, I'm making it. Not really something to adjust to."

"I hear ya." I looked around to see if Carl was listening. He went into the kitchen for something. "I'm trying to get the money together to get you out of there. What is the total amount again?"

"The judge set bail at $250,000."

"So that would be $25,000, right? 10%?"

"Yeah, I guess. I don't know much about these things, but that what folks in here seem to say. Posting bond is a process."

"You don't worry about that; let me handle things on this end."

"Ok, thanks. Cookie you are the closest friend that I have. I'm sorry for all this."

"Sorry for what? You were just doing what you thought was right, no one can fault you for that. I know

SECRETS OF A PASTOR'S WIFE

you don't belong in there; we have to focus on the positive, that's freeing you."

"I'm ready, too. They got some big brawny looking sisters in here, who look like they play for keeps."

"Ah, that's because they do. Just hold ya head, I'm coming for you."

"Hold ya head? What's that supposed to mean?"

"Don't know, heard Tyrese say it in one of their movies when his homeboy was locked down." She burst out laughing.

"You're crazy, Cook." It was good to hear her laugh. Then I heard an abrupt click, and then her voice was no more. The reality of where she was crept back in. I had to make something happen fast.

"Who was that?" Carl entered in like a bad rainfall.

"Nobody."

"Nobody? You were on the phone for close to fifteen minutes with a nobody?"

"Damn, you're monitoring my calls now?"

"As a matter of fact, I am. Since your phone is on the family account, and I pay the bill, I have every right to look at anything regarding it. That means incoming, outgoing calls, text message, and even pictures."

"You're saying that you invade my phone if I'm not around?"

"I'm saying, if it is unattended and I have a reason to investigate, then I will.

"That's such an invasion of my privacy."

"We're married, there's no such thing as privacy." His

sarcastic idea of a marriage principle angered me to the point where I didn't even want to be in his presence.

"Really, Carl?" He just sat there with a stupid look on his face, flipping channels. I went upstairs, not knowing what to do. I needed to make some calls, but was afraid to dial anyone, fearing I'd be interrogated about the who's and why's.

After sitting on my bed for a few minutes, I realized that I had work to do if I planned to get Maxine out of jail. Maybe Carl was bluffing. He could not possibly monitor every call. Who takes the time to do that? Who is that anal? I threw caution to the wind and decided to try Sister Allen. It's a shame I had to feel like this is my own household. Well, Max and I were not too different, her calls were just collect, but mine seemed to come at a much greater cost.

"Hey, Sister Allen," I said after getting her on the second ring. "We need to meet up so we can talk."

CHAPTER 16

Adrian

YOU NEVER KNOW WHAT TO EXPECT ONCE YOU WAKE up. I opened my eyes but just rested in bed, mentally planning my day while I waited for breakfast call. I watched the early morning risers going through their routines. Some were tidying up their locker boxes, getting them ready for inspection; others were making their beds up to the institution's standards. This was Friday, but unlike other prisons this place requires you to be inspection ready throughout the week.

"Chow call! Chow call!" I returned to my cut after brushing my teeth, and then filed in with the chaotic traffic that comes with early morning breakfast call. It was nearing 5:00 AM and some of the guys rolled out of the bed as is, cold in their eyes, breath smelling like a mix between last week's garbage and the bottom of a dog's paw. Obviously, they didn't care, one way or the other. Some were not raised to take pride in their hygiene. It's a shame to see grown men so far removed from what comes naturally to men on the outside. A simple task like taking a shower or brushing teeth is a planned activity in prison. In an open dormitory environment like this one you notice everyone's habits, good or bad.

We moved single file into the chow hall as we always do for every meal. The food trays are prepared by other inmates on kitchen detail and are slid through a small window one at a time. We are then ushered to our seats at four-man tables that are lined up where we are to eat in silence. Now those are rules, but of course in prison there are guys that thrive on breaking any rule possible regardless of the consequences. Some seek attention; some just revel in the thrill of being rebellious. Whichever the case, the end result is never good.

Another rule in the chow hall is if you leave the window without something on your tray, you just lost out. However, that does not stop dudes from trying. They want everything the state has to offer.

"Hey, you didn't give me my milk, homes!" Money Mel barked into the window.

"Back away from the window, inmate!" The burley officer shouted at Mel, causing everyone to notice. Money ignored the orders; he had one purpose, getting the milk he felt he deserved. After receiving the milk, he walked past Officer Stevens with an ice-grilled expression, daring him to say something.

Money Mel had a little size on him, standing at 6'2, weighing about 225 lbs. muscled up from 10 years and some change of working out. The officer wasn't but 6'o and was outweighed by close to 30 lbs., so to risk embarrassment by confronting Mel would be unwise. Mel wasn't to be intimidated by anyone; he had a reputation of causing major bodily harm to so-called dorm buddies. He was about the money and stood up to anyone getting in the way of him making his paper.

He had plenty of sense though, choosing his battles carefully. This particular morning, he refused to let some things go. Mel sat down at the table trying to enjoy the rest of his cereal. He could not concentrate because of the man sitting at the neighboring table owing him some money for quite a while. It was not a whole lot. But for Money Mel, money owed is money lost, and he hated to lose anything.

"Say Jug, what you gonna do about that paper? It's been a few weeks now." He spoke in a low tone, but loud enough for others to hear.

"Quiet down over there and eat your food!" ordered Ms. Graham, a female officer assigned to the chow hall. She was one of those who thought they could handle men because she put on a uniform. She was soft as cotton.

"Damn, Mel, why you frontin' on me up here," Jug pleaded. "I got you. You know that."

"Got me? That's what you been saying for the longest and I still got nothing." His voice was already deep and husky, so it did not take much for it to carry. "I'm tired of waiting, Jug, gimme me."

"Man, you trippin'. I'm gonna shoot you something,"

he said, nonchalantly blowing Mel off, at least that's how he took it.

"Bitch, you must think I'm playing with you!" Mel shouted as he stood to his full height. Now I've seen scenes like this before and I was glad I was near a door. It's always best to be aware of your surroundings at all times and make sure you have a means of escape in case of an emergency.

Jughead was no chump and had an established reputation himself, something he planned to protect. Although he was shocked by Mel's sudden action, he wasn't showing fear. Using the word "Bitch" in the joint is like pressing the "FIGHT" button in most guys. I'll say most because there are some guys who don't allow words to trigger them into action, then there are some who are cable ready, and it doesn't take much to charge them up.

"Who you calling a bitch?" Now Jug was talking and standing at the same time. He always rolled with a crew of dudes who were all from Baltimore, ready to go. That did not deter Mel a bit, he always held his own.

"You nigga, what ya gonna do? Huh?" His next motion was to duck the punch thrown by Jug, and then all hell broke loose. Jug's crew jumped over nearby tables to get a crack at Mel, who was defending blows from Jughead. A dude named Prime snuck Mel with his breakfast tray. The hard plastic caused a deep gush by his jaw, but with all the adrenaline rushing through him he hardly felt it or noticed the flow of blood spilling off his face.

"Hey! Hey!" Ms. Graham hollered meaninglessly. The mêlée had already ensued, food was flying, bodies were landing on tables, falling on the floor, and being tossed into innocent bystanders. Most who have been around this before knew to fall back to a wall and watch the show. Mr. Stevens, the once extra tough officer who initially confronted Mel at the tray window was in total shock; his panic caused him to delay in calling the code.

"10-10! 10-10! All units to the West chow hall! 10-10 in progress!"

It was almost too late; Money Mel was doing his best but was outmanned. A few of his partners came to his aid when they saw the odds weren't in his favor, but the damage had already been done. By the time the back-up officers showed up, Mel was lying unconscious with blood all around him. Apparently, one of Jug's crew was packing a shank and had stuck Mel with it; there was no other explanation for all the blood loss.

The medical staff showed shortly after they were called. They put Mel on the gurney while other medical staff assisted with the injured inmates. The whole incident would cause movement to be shut down until they escorted everyone back to their dorms, lock us down, and then began to clean and sterilize the eating area.

Finally, after two hours of movement halted, we came off lockdown and were able to go to detail. By the time I got to counseling, Chief had a ton of things for me to do. It was not even 10:00 and I felt like I had already put in a full day. A little early morning disturbance does not stop progress in the administration's eyes. Because we're in an assisting position, inmates have a major part in things getting done around here.

I got most of my preliminary duties taken care of before I started on the floor. I could see Pam in her office, glancing up periodically to see what I was doing. I stay engrossed in my work, not wanting to change from my normal activity. It was good that I was busy that way I could stay focused and not let my mind drift.

Victory in Faith Baptist Church was returning tonight, and all I could think about was whether that pretty woman was going to be with them. I was also concerned about security. After what happened this morning, it would be easy for them to cancel the service for fear of something breaking out up there and putting the visitors in danger. They had a good point because with situations like that you never know about the threat of retaliation.

Even though Pam and I have been talking ever since the day she brought the phone, I've still been anticipating the church coming back. I felt like a kid through the month of December watching the calendar waiting on Christmas. I could not fully understand my feelings. I had a bird in the hand yet was intrigued by the unknown bird in the bush.

"What's going on with you?" asked Pam, having a brief moment alone with me.

"Nothing, just working. Got a lot to do today, that lockdown really put me behind."

"I know it did. I enjoyed our conversation, too," she said being non-descriptive.

"That's what's up." I kept it short like I told her I would. She thought I was joking, but I've got to drive for the both of us.

"Damn, it's like that?" She turned on her heels before I could get a word out. It was cool, I would explain later. She had to learn to turn the emotion switch off when we're at work, especially since we have a way to communicate, that was the whole purpose.

I finished everything up and got prepared to go. I made sure that her office was the last stop for trash pickup before I left. When I was sure no one was looking, I caught her eye. "Everything alright?"

"Yeah, I guess." She tried to stay focused on her work, but her eyes met mine against her will. I'll call you when I'm sure you're home." She smiled which made me feel better.

I was anxious to get back. I had to eat, take a shower, and then get ready for church. Look how things have changed. I am looking forward to church like it's a date. In a sense it is, a date with destiny.

CHAPTER 17

Cookie

FRIDAY IS USUALLY CONSIDERED THE MOST STRESS-FREE day of the week. The close of the work week, and the beginning of the weekend. Reecie was looking forward to this day on her calendar. She had finally made it to varsity cheerleader and was cheering for the basketball team. As a freshman, she had accomplished something most girls her age could not. All the dance and gymnastic lessons were paying off and I was immensely proud.

For the first time in a while, we went out as a family, Reecie, Chloe, and I. Carl, like always, found himself cooped up in his office at the church. And like always, I had to soothe Reecie's disappointment by encouraging her to do her best. As long as I was there, she could get over the absence of her father.

Chloe had her own agenda for riding to the school. Though we left together, rode in the car together, even sat together, we were definitely in two different places mentally. Her focus was on the play of her beau, Gabriel, that we were not supposed to know about. With this being an afternoon game, I did not mind her mixing it up with her girlfriends while they gawked at the boys. It was harmless; besides, I was the same at her age.

I remained busy on my phone between breaks in the action. My message for the evening was stored on there, I just had to fine tune some things before I met up with the rest of the group for the ride to the prison. After finding a topic, I built my confidence by rereading what I had written.

Gabriel Measures was a good ball player, and I could understand why Chloe was taken by him. I just wanted her to be careful; there are dangers that came from being with a guy like him. But it was not something I could just come out and tell her because she chose to sneak and see him. A parent can tell when things change with their children. Chloe's mood had changed since she's been in contact with this young man. I will step in if need be, but growth comes from experience, so for now, I'm going to let her learn on her own.

Reecie was out there doing her thing. She started out looking nervous, not really keeping up with the other girls, but after a while, she fell right in step. I was proud of her, she stayed, determined to make it, not allowing obstacles to impede her path. This could lead to big things for her in the future. Like I said, experience is the best teacher.

Periodically, I look down at my phone to peruse my

notes. I saw a missed call from Sister Allen and quickly returned it.

"Hey, I'm sorry I missed your call. I'm at a basketball game with my girls. What's up?"

"I've got that information for you," she said. I knew what she was talking about so there was no need to go into detail just in case someone on her end was listening. I looked to see what Chloe doing before I responded, teenagers are naturally nosey and love to gossip.

"$25,000 right? Ok, Imma send you the info for the bail bondsman and you can make the transfer."

"Girl, I really owe you for this."

"Just glad to have accounting skills and was able to hide some funds in accounts that your husband doesn't even know about. We took in a large number of offerings this quarter and he has no plans to spend it anytime soon."

"That's good. Thanks for the work; I had to pull some drastic measures to get my friend out. Ah…I gotta go, I'll talk with you later." I ended the call when I caught Chloe straining to pick up on my conversation. She tried to play it off, but she could not hide it. I acted natural continuing to cheer on Reecie.

The game ended with a win for the home team. Gabriel had a fantastic game and was receiving accolades from his friends and teammates. We went to meet Reecie to congratulate her as well. Chloe struggled to keep sight of Gabriel, with the exciting crowd, it was tough to find anyone. However, I had a clear view of him and what I saw was disturbing.

One of his friends reached in his thick leather bomber and slid Gabriel a shiny, chrome 9mm pistol. He dapped him up then rushed out the door without another word to anyone, including Chloe. She saw him leaving and opened her mouth to call out, but nothing was audible.

"Boys are just like that, Chloe. Hell, men do thoughtless things too and we as women have to learn that they are who they are."

"I don't know what you're talking about," she said, still protecting her innocence. *If she doesn't know that I know by now, then she's fooling herself.*

"Right, let's get out of here. I must get to the church to catch the van. Your father will bring you home with him."

"Mom, are you going back to that place where the bad guys are?" Reecie asked.

"We're going to the prison, yes. And it's a place that needs God's Word. I'm just a messenger."

"Were you scared?"

"At first, then once you see how they love the Lord just as much as we do, you see that they're really not that different."

❦

"How long do you think we can keep seeing each other like this? What happens if your wife finds out?"

"She won't as long as we don't get sloppy, like calling me at home."

"It was to your cell number, damn. You gonna keep beating me up about that?"

"Yup, until you take things as serious as I am. I have a lot to lose over here."

"And I don't?"

"I didn't say you didn't."

"We have risks on both sides. So, yes, I will be more careful."

"Thank you. Now I'm outta here, my wife is bringing the kids soon, then she's heading out to the prison for service. I'll drop the kids off, and then come back."

"You sure?"

"I'm always sure about what I do."

※

We showed up at the prison a bit late due to traffic. It was alright because the prison had some sort of incident earlier and they had to put extra security in place for us. I was a little worried at first, and then I realized that they probably go through this often, and this was just a formality. We got clearance, and then came through like the last time.

Once we got the equipment set-up and the inmate musicians tune them up, we were ready to rock the house with some good old-fashioned church. The choir did a couple of songs, which got us in sync. Then we did one together as the general population filtered in. It felt good to sing with the guys, knowing we were all doing it for the same purpose, giving praise.

I could not help but focus on the door, waiting to see if Adrian was coming tonight. I know it was wrong of me to have these feelings towards another man, but how are we to know where the heart leads us. Attraction comes in some interesting packages, and there was no particular store that it's displayed in. A place as unlikely as prison can hold some of the most hidden treasures.

Everyone quieted as Minister Powers stepped to the podium to a huge round of applause. It was apparent they remembered him from the last visit a month ago. I thought it was amazing when a messenger has an impact on people; Brother Powers had left a deep impression on these men.

"Thank you, thank you. We have someone special for you this evening. Evangelist Sandra Andrews will deliver a powerful word, something to uplift and enlighten. I must warn you, she's a teacher of the word, so she knows her stuff. Let me pray you in, then turn things over to your speaker."

He gave a hair-raising prayer to usher in the spirit, preparing the way for me. After a brief introduction, I made my way to the mic.

"How you guys doing tonight? Are you ready for a strong word?" They cheered loudly. "What about a healing word? How about a loving word? I know you want a word that will free you." Everyone was on their feet, hands up praising God. "The God I serve is a deliverer and he can deliver you too. You must have just a little faith. You can have your seats." Some still remained standing, feeling the power of the Holy Spirit.

"I want to talk about the tongue, and how powerful words are. Now I know in a place like this, words are used like weapons, ready to tear someone down." I saw guys nodding their heads in agreement. "How often do you use words to pick someone up, encourage them a little bit? The Word says there is life and death spoken from the tongue. It would be foolish for me to believe that everything is all peaches and cream in here. I know you fight, argue, and curse each other out, any sort of expression to prove your manhood. Men, you have to be careful about what you say and how you say it."

"In James 3 it explains just how dangerous the tongue is. In verse 5 it says "the tongue is but a little member but boasts great things. With a little spark it can cause a blazing fire." Does this make sense to you? I know you've seen a basic quarrel turn into a full-scale fight which began over nothing." I saw some of the guys chuckling, which meant that I spoke some truth. "The tongue was created to praise, however we as man, have found another use for it, cursing. It clearly states "can salt and freshwater flow from the same stream? Can fig leaves bear olives? So why do we bless and curse with the same tongue? We've been doing it so long; we probably don't have an answer. It's become an unconscious act. I understand that it's not easy, especially in here, to think about what you say. Just think about how many fights would be avoided if every word was accounted for. What if you thought about what effect your words had on others? Something to think about." The quiet told me that their minds were open. I don't do a lot of shouting; I like to get right to the point then have you ponder.

"Every word spoken should have a meaning and a purpose. If it's not used to uplift, then you are not working how God intended for your tongue to be used. Use your words wisely and speak life instead of death. You'll be surprised at how God blesses you when you give praise."

I stepped away to a warm response. They were looking hungry, like they wanted more. We sang a couple of praise songs, prayed for anyone receiving Christ for the first time, and then did the benediction. Tonight, we did something different than the last time. We actually got a chance to shake the brother's hands as they exited. One by one, they lined up and came by the podium, greeting each of our members.

That's when I saw him. He was clean and neatly dressed just as I remembered him before. As he came closer, I suddenly became a ball of nerves. We were face to face and all I could do was smile. He extended his hand, and I took it in mine with a professional shake. He held onto my hand, which did not offend me at all. Adrian's smile was addictive, something I definitely wasn't expecting to affect me the way it did.

"You did a good job," he said leaning in to speak over all the chatter around. I kind of moved him to the side from the others who were trying to get to Brother Powers. "Excuse me," he politely apologized for brushing up against me to avoid another inmate.

"It's Adrian, right?" He was very shocked to hear me

say his name especially his first. I did not know his last so that's what I've been holding on to.

"Yes, how do you know?"

"I remember you coming up last time and giving your testimony, very powerful."

"Why thank you. Maybe we will get a chance to speak again soon, Ms. Andrews."

"Mrs. Andrews," I corrected out of habit but really wasn't intended for him.

"Alright, Upshaw, you can let her hand go now and make it back to your building." The guard wasn't being disrespectful but stern enough to let him and us know who was in control. It was a cold dose of reality. For a moment it seemed like he wasn't here, and I wasn't there. We made a connection by merely holding hands.

"You be encouraged, Upshaw," I called out. "Until next month." He gave me a knowing look. I shook a couple more hands before we departed.

In the van, my mind was full. I wondered how the guys had received me. Brother Powers had set the bar high; you could tell by the fanfare at the close of service. My spirit felt right, like I have done what I was set to do. The only one I need to please is God.

I checked my pockets to make sure I did not leave anything at the desk when I collected my keys, cell phone, and jewelry from the checkpoint. When I placed my keys in my jacket pocket , I felt a piece of folded paper that was not there before. I wondered what it was as I unfolded it.

'Call me, 301-626-0045' was written in small print.

Immediately, I smiled. How sly of him, and when did he have time to do that? Then I remembered him brushing up against me. In that split second he was able to get the paper in my jacket pocket. Oh, he's good and I liked how he operated. Confident and risky at the same time. I gotta let him know about himself when I call him. I do intend to call; it's just a matter of when.

CHAPTER 18

Adrian

"MAN DID YOU HEAR WHAT HAPPENED TO BENZO LAST night?" Preach came into my cut like he was Jim Vance, the newscaster from nightly news.

"I was at church last night, then I came back and went to bed," I didn't want to tell him I was over here on the phone. Only a few people know I have one. He has an idea that I have one but doesn't know when I pull it out or put it up. I keep everyone in the dark.

"It was really late before lockdown. He tried to rob a dude for his phone and the dude bucked, stabbing Bonzo like 15-20 times. They said he didn't make it. They got the dorm on lockdown and all yellow taped off like a crime scene."

Damn, I was so lost in my own world that I missed what was going on around me.

"What the fuck happened, man? I just talked to him

the other day on the yard, he did seem a little stressed but not to the point where he would rob anyone."

"Well, from what Chedda was sayin, Benzo was chillin' over there in E3; he had a phone contract and everything."

"Who was he trying to rob?"

"Miami Slim."

"What? Man, I heard about that dude. He used to be in our dorm. He used to rent his flip out over here too but would flake out on dudes even though they had paid for their time. I think that's real disrespectful to handle business like that, you can create enemies doin' that shit."

"I bet that's what ticked Bonzo off."

"Probably did. Preach, I can't believe he's gone.

"I know, man. E3 will be on lockdown for about a week."

"Yeah, and Miami Slim got a body charge now."

"I don't know about that; he was in his dorm defending himself. They'll take that into consideration. He'll be in the hole until he goes to free world court."

"The way the system is, he'll probably get off."

I sat back on my bunk after Preach left and wondered how it would be to not ever come home from this. You come in with the intentions of doing your time and then being released but there are so many obstacles in between. The end is not promised to anyone. I feel for his folks, to lose a son in prison is a lot to take.

The vibration startled me back to consciousness. I

went behind the makeshift partition and answered the call.

"What's up?"

"Hello, is this Adrian?" the soft mature sounding voice questioned.

"Who's asking?"

"This is Evan. Sandra Andrews slid me your number last night."

Wow! It worked. I was taking a big chance hoping she didn't throw it away. Now I'm gonna have some fun with her.

"I don't know what you're talking about. I gave you this number?"

"Maybe you didn't, and I have the wrong number. I'm sorry to bother–"

"Wait! Don't hang up; I was just playing with you. How are you?"

"I'm fine. Listen, this was probably a bad idea. I'm not into games, I'm a grown woman.

"I hear you, grown woman. What made you call, anyway?"

"Call it curiosity. I almost threw the piece of paper away, and then I thought about how bold you were to even try something like that. If the wrong person saw you, it could've gotten messy."

"Believe me, I think before I do anything. The only thing I was really worried about was whether you would call or not."

"I thought about it all night, then something happened, and I was like, why not?"

"And what was that?"

"Long story, nothing worth talking about right now. So, how are you able to have a phone in there? I'm sure they're not handing them out like issued clothing."

"You don't know about prison, do you?"

"Not really."

"There's a lot to this, just like there's a lot to me."

"I'm interested in learning."

"Are you really?"

"Yup," she said playfully.

"Well, let's talk then." And we did, for the rest of the evening. Count time came and went. We got off, got back on, switched subjects, laughed, got serious, and even shared personal stories, all in the name of good conversation. We were lost in each other's words so long that we lost track of time. The last count of the night passed by with me under the blanket enjoying the sound of her voice. When we finally hung up, it was beginning to lighten up outside. I didn't even hear breakfast call and the guys were returning from the chow hall.

Before I went down to sleep, I put my phone in the hiding spot where I know it would be safe then got some real rest. I learned that it's hard to get any good sleep owning a phone. There are so many things that can go wrong if you are not on point. With this being my first time, I'm going to do the best I can to hold on as long as I can.

When I woke later that afternoon, they were just calling yard call for the West side dorms. I decided to go out and get a run in. It has been a couple of weeks since

I have done any cardio. Mostly I have been doing push-ups, sit-ups, and working my legs by squatting or lunging. It was beautiful outside, mid 70's, with a slight breeze, which made it very pleasant for running.

I got around the track on the first lap without exerting too much energy. My mind seemed to be moving faster than my legs. The thoughts were scattered like sand on the beach. Pam occupied a portion while Sandra was piquing my interest in ways that I did not think possible. The conversation we had flowed effortlessly, it was like reconnecting with an old friend It was strange to see how in tune we were, the more we talked, the more we found in common.

Pam on the other hand, had a more physical appeal to me. Maybe it was because I saw her every day. That could cause us to be drawn to each other. But with Sandra, or Cookie, as she prefers to be called by friends, the connection is more about mental stimulation. When you can gain a person's interest through mere conversation. That has more value that a person's physical presence.

I to admit my attention was not to just one, but both women. They both fulfilled something within me, something different from each. I was eager to learn more about both of them to figure out where they fit in my life. I certainly was not trying to make a choice at this stage, they both served a purpose helping with this time I was doing.

As I rounded lap number three, I noted how the yard is sectioned off. The Hispanics were engaged in a physical soccer game where all you could hear was the shouting back and forth in their native tongue. On the basketball court, the ballers were doing the same, exchanging their own dialogue. The workout crew walked from station to station of workout equipment flexing their newly tightened muscles, competing for attention.

It was kind of humorous to see the different personalities at work. The yard was your chance to put everything on display. Everybody had something they were dealing with. That's part of doing time, it is how you deal with it that shows your true character. Some run like me, others work out to relieve stress, playing sports, reading, cleaning, washing clothes, reading, all these are coping methods used to deal with the rigors of incarnation.

Before I knew it, yard call was over, only an hour outside almost seemed unfair. The disappointment was written all over everyone's faces as they made the long walk to exit the yard. For me, I was glad to get a mile and some change in. I have learned to plan ahead before going out, if you are gonna play ball, play ball, the same applies to whatever your purpose was foregoing in the first place.

The line for the shower was as long as the one at the Six Flags for the latest ride. In a way I was glad, not because I wanted to stay sweaty, but because I had a chance to get into my spot while everyone was cleaning up. To keep others out of your business, you must be strategic. Being nosey was as natural as breathing for some people, so it's best not to give them something to see.

Once in the clear, I turned on the phone and saw a few messages. A couple of them were from Pam telling me she had something to show me Monday morning when I got to detail. I needed to fill her in on the latest also, but did not want to do it over the phone, so I too, was eager to talk with her. There was another text message from Cookie which surprised me. I was not sure I would hear from her this soon, especially since we just pulled an all-nighter.

I texted her back a brief reply, and she sent me a quick response telling me that she was free for a moment.

"I wasn't expecting to speak with you today; honestly, I was content with the high I was on."

"Really, wow, I'm flattered. Are you trying to mock me?"

"Well, if you're putting yourself in a position to be mocked."

"I wouldn't say all that Not really my style."

"Tell me a little more about your style. What makes you sounique?"

"And why are you so interested? I mean, you're handsome and obviously pretty smart so why do you want to spend time talking to me?"

"For one, you are correct; I am smart, smart enough to know what I like. I was very attracted to you when I first saw you.

"Ok, and..."

"And I believe you were attracted to me in the same way. I just acted on my attraction."

"You did what a man does when he's attracted to a woman. But there's something I have to tell you."

"What?"

"I'm married."

"Ah... ok."

"To the Pastor of our church."

"Whoa. You mean, you're the First Lady?"

"I never really liked titles. Let's put it this way, I have a lot of responsibilities in the church."

"In the home too, evidentially, so why even call me?" I displayed a bit of anger in my voice. Now I was on a quest for answers.

"Curiosity, I guess. My life is so complex, a lot of different stresses that I encounter daily. I'm looking for something simple something that makes sense."

"I thought once you get to the point where you get married it all makes sense."

"That's not always the case, it's very complicated."

"And you wish to add another complication? It seems to me that there's more going on than you're telling me."

"I'm willing to share if you are willing to listen. I am not looking to be judged here."

"What are you looking for?"

"A friend."

CHAPTER 19

Adrian

"ADRIAN, COME HERE FOR A SECOND, I NEED TO SHOW you something," Pam said solemnly in a hushed tone.

I was working as usual, trying to get my work done as quickly as possible so I could get back to the dorm. Pam appeared to be a little upset about something; it may have been because we have not spoken since Friday.

"What's up?" I said as I stepped into her office, also making sure there were not any onlookers trying to pick up on something.

"I take it you heard about Bernard."

"Yeah, that whole thing was tragic. Just could not believe he would go that far. Not really his character."

"Well, the news gets worse. This was faxed to me late Friday." She showed me a copy of the release papers for one Bernard Brown. He was being released from Lofton State Prison this Thursday. My heart sank completely. What a change of fate. He only had to be patient for one week; instead, he acted hastily, wanting instant gratification, which caused him to lose his life. Within a week he went to meet his creator, when all he wanted was to meet his little girl face to face.

"I don't know what to say."

"It's sad. What's harder is having to tell his family, especially his child's mother who, in turn, will have to explain the unexplainable to his innocent little girl."

I was not really in the mood to hear anything else or to do any talking. "Is that it, Ms. B?" She looked shocked at my formal address.

"Ah...one more thing, nobody knows about what I showed you. My co-workers and you. So, if I hear it around the compound, I know who leaked. But I would not have revealed it to you if I didn't trust you. He was your friend, and I didn't want to keep that from you."

"Thank you, that was very considerate of you."

She looked at me strangely.

"What's going on with you?"

"Nothing. I'm good."

"Adrian, I've been around you long enough to know when something is wrong."

"Just a lot to process, you know, Benzo being gone. To die in here brings a certain reality, like this could really be the end of the road for some folks."

"That's not your story though."

"It can happen to anyone, maybe not in that way. When you wake up in the morning, you never know how the day will end."

"That's the same whether in here or out in the world."

"I guess you're right. I'll call you later."

"Please do."

There was something different about the mood in the dorm when I returned. I walked in and instantly noticed mostly everyone was wearing boots or tennis shoes instead of their usual leisure footwear. In prison, this meant war was in the air and there was a haunting quiet in the dorm that was not normal. Usually, the idle chatter created a soundtrack of serenity, that was not the case this afternoon. Everyone had gone to eat so they were pretty much in for the evening. Whatever was going on had been lingering for hours.

On my way to my bed, I felt the stares in my direction as if I were the object of everyone's attention. Preach was always the first one in my cut welcoming me in with the latest dorm gossip. But even he was not around which was out of the norm. I looked to my bunkmate for some sort of answer to what was going on, but he just rolled over on his side like he did not want to be bothered.

"Man, what's going on in here?" I asked my neighbor who I hardly spoke to.

"Bro, you'll find out soon enough," he gave me a brief answer then went back into his silence.

"Alright, 'preciate it." I shot back with the same amount of emotion.

Instead of getting into my post-detail routine, I decided it was best I stay dressed and alert for the unexpected. Unexpected is what it was when Styles and Live Wire came through. I've been knowing these two for a few years from the other dorms, we happened to reunite when they moved in here last month.

"Yo, A.U., shits in the air that you cuffin' a phone up in here. Now it's none of our business how you do your business. Me and Styles, we ain't got no beef with you but there's some new niggas in here who want in."

"Yeah, they don't think you deserve to have no phone especially if you ain't showing love."

It was dead quiet in there like everyone was waiting to hear my response. Silence was my best weapon at the moment. For one, I had to think, weigh out my options before I move.

"We just wanted you to know what was up."

"And that's why everybody is strapped up?"

"Brothers got the toolies and everything. B. you got some riders in here. Even your boy Preach back there with his boots tied up to the max. I thought he was gonna pass out for a minute because them joints was tight."

"It's no secret now, son, these dudes want to move on you. There's somebody in here who is sour because they put them on you. Probably one of these jealous mothafuckas who don't wanna see you with shit." Live Wire added.

"One thing I hate is a nothing ass nigga who sits back and plots on another nigga. That's just shallow as hell."

"What's even worse is the nigga who plays like they cool then gets down with the set up."

"Yo, that's some foul shit. The question is, what you gonna do?"

That was a good question and there was a lot riding on my decision. The answer to this question could be detrimental to a lot of people. There are people like Preach who have things to consider, his soul for one. Doing what he feels is a show of loyalty could damage his character and detour the journey that he has been for as long as I can remember. Getting into a physical altercation is in direct conflict to what he believes. Others may think he is faking it, but I believe him. An incident like this, with him involved, would do nothing but confirm what those doubters think about him. Consistency is what builds the foundation for one's character. He has done that, and I would hate for him to lose credibility by jumping in my battle.

I recognized what this is for me, nothing but a test. There is something looming for me around the corner and how I handle this will show whether I'm ready for what's in store. Now it's not easy for the prison mind to wrap itself on this way of thinking. The normal and most respected response to situations like this is action, war, retaliation, any one of these is supposed to be a vehicle of gaining respect. Anything less than that desired response will be considered a weakness.

Tough pill to swallow because with every pill, there are side effects. One thing is for sure, the decision I make will leave a lasting impression, good or bad.

"Where these dudes at? I ask calmly.

"They back in the cut. Whatever you wanna do, bro, we wit you. All you gotta do is go and you got soldiers that's gonna go. We don't like niggas that try to plot on the innocent, the ones that don't bother nobody."

"That's peace, bro. 'Preciate it."

They walked off passing by Preach who approached my cut with a different swagger. It made me chuckle to myself, but I applauded his effort trying to look tough.

"Jo-Jo told me to give you this," he handed me a 6" long piece of metal about 2" wide, sharpened at one end with a gripped handle.

Just seeing the shank flashed all kinds of horror in my mind. Over the years I have seen damage caused by such a lethal weapon. Early on in my time, I witnessed a guy get stabbed so bad that by the time the medical unit got to the scene, the blood flow was unstoppable. The assailant himself went into shock after seeing what he had done. I know firsthand that shanks are nothing to play with. Benzo learned the hard way by underestimating a man with a banger.

I looked at the piece of steel lying on my bed and thought about Benzo. I wondered if he thought his situation through before he acted. He probably would still be here. I am not going out bad moving too quickly.

"Jo-Jo gave me one too," Preach said confidently.

"You know that's not you, bro. No disrespect, but you're not built for any of this. Hell, I don't even know if I am. I'm in a different place in my life where my choices matter."

"A.U., I just want you to know I got your back."

"I know you do, Preach, and you don't need no banger to prove that."

Now I am realizing the decisions I make affect more than just me. They affect my family, who expects me to come home in one piece, my friends, and myself. Even Pam and my new acquaintance Sandra would find it hard to believe that I got caught up in some mess. It's tough knowing you have so much to lose, dealing with guys with everything to gain.

I sat down at the foot of my bed, the same space where Preach usually occupies, and said a brief prayer. I was mostly looking for direction. A clear-cut answer to my problems would have been nice, but any sign from God to know that He had a handle on the situation would be wonderful now. I opened my eyes to a sense of relief, a calm that resonated over the dorm.

My prayer must have been longer than I thought. Looking around I noticed guys were in a more relaxed frame of mind, far from the tense mood that filled the air only minutes ago. The boots and war gear were replaced house shoes and leisure shorts, wave caps and wife beaters.

Something else was missing. Evidently, the two bad boys who were coming to take my phone were now in the sally port in handcuffs, awaiting the sergeant. They were pleading their case to the floor officer on duty to no avail. I wondered how I missed the commotion of them moving out.

"You got some powerful people in your corner, bro." Preach said rushing over to me.

"What you mean, Preach?"

"Smoke and Yusef put them dudes on the door a little while ago. They gave them a choice, either leave peacefully or by force. They told them that we don't tolerate no robbing, stealing, or bullying in the dorm. You know Smoke and 'em been in this dorm the longest and what they say goes. Those new boys didn't want those types of problems, dealing with those old heads."

"People have things to lose up in here and if they came for me, it would be a lot of heat on the dorm, which we don't need. I'm glad they stepped in."

"I am too. I didn't want to hurt nobody, but I was ready."

"I saw," I said chuckling. What really had me elated inside is how I sat back and allowed God to work things out in my favor. Most who I am around don't understand the power of prayer, but I do. While my head was bowed, the spirit was being moved. I'm sure if Preach knew that I was over here praying, he would be giving me a high five. Just knowing I chose the correct course of action is praise enough for me.

CHAPTER 20

Cookie

I AM GENUINELY CONCERNED ABOUT CHLOE AND THIS little thing she has going on with Gabriel. I do not want to discredit what they have by calling it a "little thing" but they're young and she really doesn't know as much about this boy as she thinks. At that age boys will say whatever they think a girl wants to hear. The fact that he is a local basketball star just makes matters worse. To her he can do no wrong; or is it that she does not want to see the wrong, for fear that he will not want her anymore.

My job as a mom is protecting her from any form of hurt caused by teenage boys who are smelling themselves. That is why I'm out here two cars behind Gabriel and some of his cohorts, trying to find out what kind of activities he's into after school hours. I sat outside the school watching Chloe part from her friends, get ugly stares from the jealous girls when she hugged and pecked Gabriel on the lips before boarding the bus, and then focused on Gabriel and his boys as they left the parking lot.

Their departure was not hard to spot, the music coming out of the speakers caused everyone to take notice and start a makeshift parking lot party as they drove on. I allowed a couple of cars and a motorcycle to get in between us before I pulled into traffic.

The navy-blue Impala traveled down Annapolis Road, heading out of Bowie. The motorcycle sped off, leaving only two cars separating us. I tried my best to moderate my speed, not wanting to give myself away. His windows were heavily tinted, so that made it hard to tell what he could and could not see. It was best I play it safe.

Gabriel's car stayed on this stretch of road even when it crossed over 193 that would take you into Greenbelt one way and Mitchellville the other. He appeared to be heading towards Landover. Once we passed through New Carrollton, I knew my hunch was right. Even though Landover was changing its image, especially when the Redskins moved to FedEx Field which is located in the heart, it still had its rough areas.

It looked as if we were heading into one of the housing projects called Village Green. As the road changed to a single lane, I closed the distance to one car. When the Impala went deeper into the maze, I eased over to a spot where I could keep an eye on his movements. He stopped in front of a house with a small fence and a lot of kids toys in the yard.

On the porch were four other guys engaged in conversation when Gabriel walked up. There was some sort of exchange, money for a black duffle bag, its contents unknown. Whatever the case, the whole scene looked suspect. Coming out of the gate, Gabriel looked to make sure he wasn't detected. His eyes peered from right to left, and then stopped briefly in my direction before going to his car.

I started the ignition and got ready to follow him again when suddenly two cars screeched to a halt boxing me in. A man jumped out the passenger side brandishing an assault rifle pointed at my window. Another man came around to provide back up as if I was an unruly hostage. Truth be told, if they only knew how sacred I was, they'd pack their guns up and go home. At least that is what I was hoping. It didn't quite happen that way.

"Get out the car, right now!" the husky man with the Wizards ball cap ordered. I guess I moved too slowly because his partner chimed in.

"Did you hear what he said?"

"Don't make me ask you again, or I'll light this car up like the Fourth of July."

"Alright, I'm moving. Please, don't shoot." I pleaded, easing out of my vehicle.

"What are you doing around here?"

"You the cops or something?" both were battering me with questions.

"No....no I'm not the police. I know someone who lives over this way."

"Oh yeah, who?" I had to think fast. I wasn't expecting for that lie to come out but since it did, I had to cover it with another one.

"Ms. Jackson." I figured there would be a Jackson in every neighborhood.

"Bullshit!" He barked now aiming the rifle at me. "I've never seen you around here before. I believe you're spying on somebody."

A crowd formed viewing the commotion taking place. I figured this would be my saving grace, enough witnesses out here and surely, they couldn't do anything crazy. Boy, was I wrong, dead wrong.

"Hold on fam, I know her," Gabriel emerged through the crowd. "I thought I recognized that car following me. You have a lot of nerve coming down here like this. My question is, does Chloe know you're out here playing detective?"

"I just don't want you hurting my daughter with your illegal activity." I was still under fire, so I chose my words carefully.

"Illegal activity? You don't know nothing about me. I don't know what you're up to, but it sounds like you're trying to jam me up. You came this far to see what I had going on? All you had to do was ask your daughter."

"She wouldn't tell me the truth."

"Well, you could've just asked me. I saw you guys at the game the other day. Or you could've gotten the number out of her phone since you already been in there snooping around." I was in shock by his statement.

Chloe knew that I had been in her phone and didn't say anything, and then she actually told Gabriel?

"Like I said, I'm just trying to protect my daughter, by any means."

"You gotta do what you gotta do, right?"

"Right," I said confidently.

"So do I. Ya'll bag her up." And in that instant, everything went black.

※

"You wanted to see me, Pastor?"

"Yes, Sister Allen, please come in and have a seat." She walked in gingerly, not exactly sure what prompted this meeting, but had an idea.

"How can I help you?"

"Well, I was looking over the numbers for this quarter's revenue and I found something quite interesting." Now my wheels were turning.

"What's that?"

"From my reports it appears as if we're gonna get a huge blessing from the I.R.S. this year. The way that you've balanced our finances has been exceptional, and you've given me no reason to question your work."

"Why, thank you Pastor. I try hard to put my degree in accounting to work. I'm just glad it is a capacity that pleases you."

"It certainly does. Now I must warn you, this year will extremely challenging. The more we bring in, the harder it will be to keep the government out of our business. It's just the nature of the beast."

"I understand and I'll do my best."

"Another issue I want to address with you is about our Sunday offerings."

"What about them?"

"When we deposit them at the end of Sunday services, we must record them accurately. Because they're cash donations and the I.R.S. will be looking hard for us to slip up. I don't intend to, Sister Allen."

"Me either."

Maxine called Cookie numerous times with no answer. Her constant voicemail recording was frustrating. Where was her friend when she needed her? Today marked the one-year anniversary of her husband's passing and the memories were very painful. Throughout the year she hadn't had anyone to talk to, usually she is the one who does the listening.

She and Cookie had come to the point where they could share intimate details of their lives and not be judged by the other. The ultimate show of friendship came when Cookie extended her hand and pulled some strings to bail her out of jail. She knew Max did not need to be there and did everything in her power to get her out. True enough, there is a trial pending, but at least she had some time to breathe.

Today she was facing an emotional barrier that she

just couldn't see handling on the inside of a jail cell, yet she hardly wanted to do it alone. Her son was grown and on his own, at an age where his life's problems were a priority. Plus, he resented his mother when she began dating again. Torey didn't understand that Maxine needed a cure for her loneliness.

Maxine had a difficult time explaining what she was experiencing. As a young parent, how do you tell your son that his dad has terminal cancer? She could barely take it in herself. In fact, she didn't find out until she had already fallen in love with him. She decided to marry Robert Stinson despite knowing he would not be a part of her or their future child's life. For richer or poorer, in sickness and in health is what she reminded herself of every day until he took his last breath.

She tried her cell one more time and if she did not reach her this time, she would leave a detailed message. It rang twice, and then a voice answered.

"Yeah, what's up?" a man's gruff voice replied.

"I'm calling for Sandra. Where is she at? This is her phone." Max questioned whether she had the right number.

"Yeah, this is her phone. She's tied up at the moment. You can come get her from the Landover Mall parking lot. Look for her car at the south entrance." Then click, the phone went dead. Without a second thought Max was on the road headed to rescue her friend from whatever danger she was in.

CHAPTER 21

Adrian

THE PLAY IN THE PAINT WAS GETTING REAL PHYSICAL. Elbows were being thrown; bodies being tossed around all to jockey for position.

"He keeps pushing me ref!" Richie Rich screamed out.

"Stop cryin' nigga! We eatin' down here!" his opponent taunted.

"Tone it down! The both of you or I'll hit you with a double technical foul." The referee was doing his best to get control of the game. This was a championship game. True enough it was in prison, but in here we take sports very seriously. No trophies or television interviews, just bragging rights amongst our peers.

Tempers were flaring out of frustration. The game had been close up until about four minutes left in the first half. Rich was doing all he could battling the East side's big men down low, but he was our only man over

6'3. I was holding it down at the guard position, our shooting guard Goldie was knocking down shots here and there. The boards were our problem; if we did not make the basket, we had no one to help rebound. All throughout the season we made it with ease, mostly due to our full roster which we were familiar with. Then towards the end the problems came. Keith Wilkins went home, that was something we could not avoid, nor could we hate on. However, it did reduce us down to a smaller line up until Richie Rich came back from court. We were good for a few games, and then we lost Perez, the Puerto Rican King, as he refers to himself. He was a great athlete, good in all sports, even played professional baseball at one time before he got incarcerated. Because he was in our dorm, we were blessed to have him as a part of our basketball team. He had good size, 6'4, about 245 lbs., and could leap out of the gym. Perez had only one shortcoming, which was a huge problem in the eyes of prison administration. He could not control his masturbation.

Women were his weakness, the stone to this Goliath. At this facility, the female staff made up about 55-60%. That meant female officers would more than likely work your building at one point or another. And that spelled trouble for Perez; he just could not resist the lust of the flesh. Whether it was his fascination with a woman in uniform or the mere sound of their voice, something would trigger him and send him reeling, bursting with emotion that he could only release through physical stimulation.

This became the norm for Perez as he would go to the hole from different dorms around the compound for the same infraction. The warden, thought he could put an end to his addiction, locked him down for an absurd number of days in the hole and made it a standard. Perez was the first to spend over two months in isolation for a masturbation offense. The warden said that this was his "tough on exposure" law.

Being in a men's facility, doing time away from female interaction was hard for some guys. You had to find ways to release the tension. Most men would develop a workout routine to channel that energy. I like to run, others play sports to exert their physical energy, and a select few had the mental fortitude to simply block out the urge to want to be with a woman. Then there are those who have fallen weak and succumb to the urges and choose homosexual activity. They claim prison is their excuse for forging relationships with other men. To me, that excuse is as weak as their mental state. We have choices and if you choose homosexuality then that has been in you before you came in.

Our team was depleted in a major way when we lost Perez to the hole. Goldie and I could not make enough threes to overcome the run H building made before the half. We found ourselves down by 17. The warden, who just happened to be in support of our team, walked in the gym astonished by what he saw on the scoreboard. It was no secret he had made a wager with his warden over security who was backing the East side squad, so he wanted some answers.

"What's going on out there?" he questioned to no one in particular. He walked back and forth, and then directed his next question to the coach, one of the older brothers in our dorm.

"What's wrong Mingo? Ya'll can't beat those boys over there?"

"Sir, we're getting killed on the boards. We need Perez, he'd shut that shit down."

"So, you mean to tell me, if you had Perez you can win?"

"Yes, sir," he answered full of confidence.

"Ok, this is what I'll do; I'll let him out of the hole for the remainder of the game. If you guys win, he stays out and can go back into your dorm. But if you lose, I'm locking him and you up." The threat was heard throughout the bench. Now the pressure was really on. Our coach could end up going to the box depending on how we play.

"Bet that." Mingo stated forgetting that he was talking to the warden. He disregarded the tone he was addressed with and made the call.

"A-1 to J-3."

"Go for J-3," the radio squawked back.

"Release inmate Perez and have him escorted to the gym immediately."

"Yes sir, that's a 10-4."

"He'll be here shortly." The warden pulled the head referee to the side and whispered something to him. As sure as he said it, a few moments later Perez sauntered into the gym escorted by two officers. His beard had grown out like a mountain man and his hair was scraggly. He still had on his jumpsuit, which was the standard isolation gear, no tee shirt, and no socks. When he got over to the bench, he peeled off the dirty looking jumper, and stood standing there in his boxers. A player that hadn't entered the game offered up his gym shorts. The gym assistant issued him some shoes in his size, and then the referee told him to grab a jersey and to check in at the scorer's table.

Without so much as a warm-up, Perez took the court with the other starters and began the second half. After one or two times up and down the court, he found his legs and went to work. He made an immediate impact on defense when one of the East sider's came in the paint with a lay- up attempt. Perez blocked it into a fast break on the other end.

We caught a groove with Perez in the line-up and cut the lead to single digits with crisp ball movement, cuts to the basket, and high percentage shots from outside. It was like he made everything click. All those problems in the paint disappeared with his presence. Richie Rich was most relieved of all, he was now free to roam and to do what he did best, slash into the hoop.

When Perez got out on the break with me pushing the ball, everyone fell into position. I swung the ball to Rich who in turn lofted it up to Perez for a thunderous dunk that erupted the crowd who was waiting for something exciting to cheer for. They got what they wanted, that slam put us up two, and we never looked back. The game went down as one of the most memorable performances in Lofton sports history. Everyone celebrated our victory at the end of the game.

The warden kept his word and allowed Perez to stay on the compound. All the way down the sidewalk you could hear them chanting, "Da King! Da King! Da King!" Praise for the Messiah who was resurrected from the hole and lead them the to the Promise Land. Meanwhile, on the Eastside, a huge fight broke out. The blame game between players turned into a full-scale brawl that took ten officers and the whole security team to get under control.

I stepped on the walk on my way to detail the next day and received props for a well-played game. They were still talking about Perez and his legendary dunk all up front by the warden's office. He was beaming knowing he had won the bet with his peers. All was good until I returned to the dorm and saw that his bunk and lockers were empty. Perez was in the hole once again for his usual charge. I guess you can take the lion out of the jungle, but he will still be a lion wherever he goes.

"We just talked to him, Pam; I can't believe he still went to the box." I sat down with Pam when the other counselors went on their lunch break, leaving her behind. She told them she had too much paperwork to catch up on. "You should've seen the look of disappointment on the guys faces."

"Adrian some men have a problem and don't have the courage inside to fix it. Perez has a strong exterior, trust me I've met with him before, but on the inside, he is a fragile human being."

"Not everyone can have a beautiful woman to look at and flirt with all day." She came around the desk and stood in front of me, and then leaned down in my face.

"You, my handsome friend, haven't taken a look or flirted with me in I don't know how long. What's up with that?" she said noticing me glancing at her very visible cleavage spilling over her bra.

"Driving this car keeps us from crashing. The actions I take or don't take are for our own benefit."

"I know.... but what if I want you," she pouted, with her bottom lip poked out. I wanted so bad to take it in my mouth. It was very tempting, and she wasn't making it any easier. "Now what's up with all that talk you had last night on the phone?"

"Calm down, ma, you never know who is lurking around here."

"There's nobody here."

"Hello, is anyone here?" I was already on my feet when I heard the door creek open. Pam was startled a bit not expecting an intruder disturbing her groove.

"Excuse me, I was looking for counselor Crenshaw." Pam seemed irritated when she saw who it was at her door.

"Ah, I believe I heard Mr. Crenshaw tell you earlier that he would be in a meeting and that he would call you up in the morning. Now, what is it that you want, Barker?"

Brian Barker, AKA Big B around the compound, has a less than admirable reputation for being in the right place at the wrong time. Basically, he is nosey for no reason. Well, he has his reasons, and his reports usually get people jammed up. His label as a snitch has followed him from camp to camp over his long incarceration, yet it has not deterred him from reporting truths and false. Big B has been beat up, stabbed, robbed, and put on the door in most dorms, but he still comes back doing what he does. The man is relentless and I for one didn't want him in my business.

"Ms. Breston, is there any more trash in here before I take this out?" I said as I grabbed the nearly empty trash bag. She should have caught the hint and resumed her normal activity.

"No, I think that's all I have, Upshaw, thank you."

I left her with the informant, Mr. Front Page News. I just hope she knows to run him off.

"Let me get a visitation form and I'll be on my way." It sounded like a stall tactic, so I decided to rescue her from the situation altogether.

"Oh, I'm glad you reminded me, Big B, I need to fill one out too. Damn, I remember Ms. Staples was supposed to make those copies earlier, but I don't think she got around to it. When you come up in the morning, I got you, B.".

"Oh, ok, cool. Thanks, A.U. I'll check you in the morning."

"That's what's up."

I heard the door click shut and a sigh of relief fell from Pam.

"Thank you."

"I got your back."

"I see that."

"Let me get outta here before you have some more unexpected company."

"Does that mean I get a rain check?" she asked seductively,

"As long as the sky forms clouds, there's always a chance for rain."

"Oh, you got jokes." I just winked at her on my way out.

CHAPTER 22

Cookie

I FOUND MYSELF TRYING TO FIGURE OUT MY WAY IN the dark. After those goons put that black sack over my head, I did everything I could to fend them off. I believe I caught one or two of them when I went to swinging wildly. Their strength was too much for me and eventually I was forced into the trunk of my own car.

The vehicle began moving, and that caused me to be concerned. I did not have a clue where we were heading or where I would end up. I didn't really know whether I would live or die. Things were getting serious all because I wanted to be nosey, getting in this man's business. As we were riding to who knows where, I started thinking about how I got in this position in the first place. Even more important, how was I gonna get free.

I saw images of Reecie and Chloe, images of my patients in need, images of the church family, even an image of Carl and our history flashed before me. I was surprised to see an image of Adrian, a man I had hardly met, but intrigued me enough to pursue a friendship. With all of these different reasons to live, I went into a place where I knew would bring me peace, prayer. I opened up to God, confessing my wrong doings and expressing my will to live for my family and friends.

While crying out to the Lord, the car stopped. Truthfully, I don't know how long we had been motionless, but I was grateful. One of my prayers was to bring this nightmare to an end. I thought my images had vanished until a vision of Max calling my name came in crystal clear.

"Cookie! Cookie! Are you ok?" I could hear her now and she sounded so close. The light blinded my eyes when the black hood was snatched off and Max's face appeared. "Let me get you out of there."

"Max! Am I glad to see you. How did you know where to find me?"

"I called your phone like a hundred times and finally this guy answered and was rude as hell. He told me where to pick you up. I don't think whoever did this wanted to hurt you."

"What makes you say that?" I said, dusting myself off, straightening my clothes from the rough ride. I looked around and realized where I was. I knew the Landover Mall parking lot very well, just wondering why they chose there of all places.

"Look at you. Besides your hair is tossed around a bit, you're in good shape." Max inspected me from head to toe. "You have some blood around your fingernails."

"Yeah, I clawed a couple of them dudes before they scooped me up. I wasn't trying to go out like that, not without a fight."

"Well, look at the First Lady out here scrapping with some thugs."

"I ain't always been in the church. Had I been packing like I used to when I was with Terry back in the day, there may be some dead brothers around the way."

"At least you're not dead because it could've turned out for the worst."

"Amen to that."

I followed Maxine to her office where we sat, had some tea, and decompressed. The events over the past couple of days had been a little overwhelming for the both of us. She filled me in on everything regarding her late husband and her strained relationship with her son. I had no idea she had such a difficult past. She needed to vent just as much as I did, if not more. She explained why she decided to get into therapy. Helping others was a way to help herself.

I wasn't ready to go home just yet. It seemed like trouble surrounded the place where I rest my head. The only bright spot was seeing Reecie's smiling face. She was oblivious to the dark moods that filled the air around her. As she would get older, the different ways to love will become apparent. My job is to show her the purest form of love, the one from a mother's heart.

Carl and I just don't see the world the same. His view is distorted, only cleared by the work he does at his beloved church. The energy he puts into his work there is not equaled at the place where his family dwells. The man is the head of his household, so if the leader is not standing up to the responsibilities, then the home will be unstable. A rocky foundation leads to rocky times, and that's where we're at.

"The last time we really had a chance to speak, you were telling me about a certain young man that had your attention." Instantly, I smiled at the mentioning of Adrian. It dawned on me that I hadn't returned his missed calls. My phone was left under the driver's seat, along with the keys that enabled Max to open the trunk where I was. I checked in with everyone except him.

"Yeah, he's pretty cool, but we're just getting to know each other. I'm still trying to soak it all in. Right now, it's awkward and talking is not the easiest, but we're working it out. It's about timing and we have to get ours down."

"Sounds like you're willing to make an effort."

"I am."

"Is it worth it? That's the question you have to ask yourself."

"Are you asking if it's worth risking my marriage? I don't think having a friend is all that bad considering where Carl and I are at. I'm at the point where I'm seeking happiness, so we'll see."

"Hey, I'm all for happiness. Just be careful."

"I'm good with that. My concern is for Chloe. This guy Gabriel is more serious than even she realizes, and I really don't think he has her best interest in mind. He has some skeletons in his closet that he doesn't want to be let out. I saw him make an exchange, money for a black duffle bag."

"What was in the bag?"

"Don't know, really. But I know it has to be something fishy going on."

"You don't know for sure. Remember what happened to me and what I'm going through before you go speculating. I would sit Chloe down and see what she knows about him."

"I tried, she's in such denial, and it's hard to get through to her."

"You have to keep trying, for your daughter's sake. If there's any truth to what you saw, she could be in danger too, much worse than what you went through."

"You're probably right."

"A mother's love for her daughter can overcome any obstacle. Use your power."

"Thank you, friend."

I took Maxine's advice and went home to speak with Chloe. On my way, I decided to try Adrian. He had been on my mind since we had our last conversation. His disposition was pretty laid back considering where he was at. If I were in his position, I don't think I would be that cool. None of us are built the same and that was evident with him.

"Is this Adrian?" I asked cautiously.

"Who's calling?"

"Sandra Cooke."

"Oh hey, how are you? Long time no hear."

"I know, I know. I saw your calls, just couldn't get to the phone at that time."

"I understand. It's like that on my end sometimes. For me, it's either the police are walking through or I haven't gotten the phone out yet."

"Do you always answer your phone like that?" I was curious.

"I'm always cautious of who could be calling. In here it's better to be safe than sorry. People play all kinds of games, the officers too."

"Officers have your number?" The question sounded stupid the moment I asked it. He chuckled.

In some cases if you're sloppy your number can fall into the wrong hands. Especially if someone wants to see you get knocked off, they will give your math up to the folks."

"What? Were you just speaking English? I didn't catch a word you said."

Adrian burst out in a full laugh.

"My bad, those were phrases we use in here. Getting 'knocked off' means to lose what you have, "math" is the number, and the 'folks' are the officers or police."

"Hold on, I'm taking this down." I joked, which got him on his heels.

"You serious?"

"Naw. Just playing with you, but I will need a cliff note version of our conversations if I'm ever tested."

"I'll try to remember that."

"Have you been knocked up before?"

His laugh boomed in my ear.

"You mean knocked off and no, thank God. There have been some close calls though. I've seen guys lose and it's not a pretty sight. You sure have a lot of questions about what goes on in here, you plan on paying us a visit?"

"I believe I already do. I'm interested in the things I can't see. The things the television exaggerates so who's better to give me the real scoop than you?"

"That's admirable. Not many want to know anything about us. We are considered a lost breed of people to most in the world, not really 20/20 material. You trying to be my Barbara Walters?"

"Ha, Ha, funny. Just want to know more about you, that's all."

"Nothing wrong with that. So why don't you come and see me then?"

"I try to see you when I come with the church."

"I'm talking about a personal visit."

"Personal visit? Is that possible? I mean, I'm associated with the church, they may have restrictions on that."

"Well, it won't hurt to ask. I work for the counselors who do the approvals."

"You got the hook-up, huh?"

"I ain't saying all that. I could check on it though. But you never answered my question."

"And what's that?"

"Do you want to come see me?"

"If you can arrange it, I think I'd like that. I'll have to work out some things on my end."

"You mean with your husband?"

"Yes, how did you know?"

"Because I'm sure you have to get things cleared."

"Cleared?" I was offended. "Not the case at all. Just making sure I'm careful with how I move. My situation is delicate."

"I can imagine. I promise to handle with care."

"Do you keep your promises?"

"Always."

"We'll see when I get there."

I saw a number flash across the screen of my phone that was not familiar. At first, I thought to ignore it fearing it was a telemarketer or someone trying to collect. But against my better judgment I answered anyway.

"Hello."

"I see you've been freed. That's good; my intentions weren't to hurt you, just to scare you a bit. Be careful when dealing with people you don't know. Your daughter doesn't know about what happened to you. But since you are a praying woman, I pray she won't find out. It would be in the best interest of you and your whole family. This is not a threat but a warning to not try and figure out my business dealings. Leave well enough alone." Then there was silence. I just listened the whole time, knowing all too well who was on the other end. Gabriel made his message loud and clear.

The odd sounding chime caught my attention, alerting me that an email was coming through. I went to the desktop and saw that it was a church bulletin advertising a spring concert that the choir would be performing. It was one of those blanket emails that everyone in the community receives. I minimized it and noticed an opened email behind it.

Carl had been communicating with someone and I guess this was their reply. I read the first line in disbelief: *I've been trying to find ways to control my feelings towards you but it's getting harder by the day. You avoid my calls, ignore my attempts, and then deal with me only on your terms. I know you have a wife and I've tried to be understanding. This thing that we've been calling a friendship is just not enough for me, I need more, I want more and I'm going to do what I gotta do in order to move this friendship into something more.*

After reading the email, I maximized the church bulletin to cover up his secret. I was speechless. Over the 15 years of marriage, I never had a reason to suspect Carl of cheating. It's amazing how one email can change everything.

I had so many questions but did not want to ask Carl one single thing. No, I would just watch him, let my anger subside, and then wait for the guilt to eat him alive. The best weapon against a cheating husband is a word unspoken. Revenge is best served cold.

CHAPTER 23

EVERY NOW AND THEN IN THE JOURNEY THROUGH life, you want to know the truth. Once you learn the truth, then you want to share your truth with everyone else. Living all these years in the shadows has been difficult, almost to the point where I lost my sanity. I chose life over death and ended up finding a purpose for my truth.

My mother told me growing up to be the best man I can be and do not let anyone tell me I couldn't achieve greatness. She encouraged me, she empowered me, she supported me through all my endeavors, and then she disappointed me by hiding the details of her failed relationship with my father. To me, that was too much like lying. When a parent lies, it seems like it does something to you. For me, it knocked me down, making it hard to get up.

I never had a chance to find closure with my mother.

She died in a horrible car accident taking her guilt with her to the grave, probably not resting in peace knowing her son had resented her until her premature end. The remainder of my adult years were spent forging my own way into manhood.

I saw pictures of my father but never had a chance to meet him. Heard stories about him but could not recall one single experience with my parents together. For a long time, I operated like I was fatherless, however there comes a period in life when you go looking for answers. Maybe those answers could explain why I could not achieve the greatness my mother said I was destined for.

Instead, drug addiction sucked me in like the newest model Hoover vacuum. Between rehab and brief jail stints, my life became a tumultuous roller coaster. When the weed high was not enough, cocaine took its place and fulfilled the satisfaction. When I couldn't afford a fix or a good meal, I'd commit a senseless crime just to get arrested. Maybe public drunkenness, disorderly conduct, or a shoplifting charge would get me a good night's sleep and a hot meal.

Life was really doing a number on me, hitting me with blows that Holyfield, Lenox Lewis, and Tyson would marvel at. I took them all, got knocked down more than I care to admit, but did not let life knock me out. Fighting back hasn't been easy as it called for a mental fortitude only found in soldiers. That's what I considered myself, a soldier of fortune, the fortune I was striving for was a life more abundant. That could only come by living in a way pleasing to God.

I beat my addiction. Got off the powder, gave up the trees, and started searching for the true meaning of life. A life sober was a life of clarity and I was better for it. Getting back on track was as difficult as driving a car with four flat tires. I needed help in a major way. The spirit was drawing me to seek the help; the road was leading me to a destination that brings hope, joy, and peace. The door that said "Welcome all you who are weak and heavy laden" was Victory in Faith Baptist Church.

As I walked down the aisle, I could feel the energy engulf me. The choir sounded angelic, and the congregation was all afoot chanting, singing, jumping, and praising their God to the highest. I loved the atmosphere already, but would they love me? I kept an open mind because there was no coincidence for why I was here. There was a calling on my life. A testimony was being completed by my presence there today. I had passed the test now it was time to talk about it with hopes that my story would help someone else overcome.

Overcomers make it through something. I made through the storm, faced adversity, challenged by hardship, and recovered admirably. The only thing left to do was to be an inspiration. For special testimonies, a platform is built. What better platform to reintroduce myself to the world than the pulpit that the famed Carlton Andrews built? Who better to step to him with the greatest confession of all, in front of his whole church family? His son, Carlton Andrews Jr.

I stood face to face with the man whose eyes looked

like mine, smile that gave birth to mine. Though at this moment, he was not in a smiling mood. He was trying to figure how, when, and why did I choose today to become that thorn in his side. Like Paul, God's grace is sufficient. But could he perform with grace as the church he was pastoring looked on in awe at this awkward meeting? It was time for answers. It was time for the truth. "Hello, dad, I have returned."

To be continued

ABOUT THE AUTHOR

Billie Miff is not just a name but a mindset I have adopted while being faced with countless adversities. The process of writing stories creates the right mindset for the reader.. A Billie Miff classic will take the reader into familiar places, introduce characters that are easily relatable, and experience events that put things into another perspective. That is the power of creativity, it opens the mind up to all possibilities, where any ending can be your ending. Whether it is a Happily Ever After or a tragic conclusion, Billie Miff always leaves the reader wanting more than the page before. The body may be locked, lost in its own essence but the mind Is forever free. That is the hidden meaning of Billie Miff... where every book written is a classic.

Made in the USA
Columbia, SC
01 May 2025